Trace

Dawn Sullivan

MW00957840

All rights reserved. No part of this publication may be reproduced, stored in a retrieval system, or transmitted in any form or by means mechanical, electronic, photocopying, recording or otherwise without prior permission from the author. This is a work of fiction. Names, characters, places and events are fictitious in every regard. Any similarities to actual events or persons, living or dead are purely coincidental. Any trademarks, service marks, product names or featured names are assumed to be the property of their respective owners and are used only for reference. There is no implied endorsement of any of these terms are used. Except for review purposes, the reproduction of this book in whole or in part, mechanically or electronically, constitutes a copyright violation. Published in the United States of America in January 2015; Copyright 2015 by Dawn Sullivan. The right of the Authors Name to be identified as the Author of the Work has been asserted by them in accordance with The Copyright, Designs and Patent Act of 1988.

Published by Dawn Sullivan
Cover Design: Kari Ayasha-Cover to Cover Designs
Photographer: Shauna Kruse-Kruse Images & Photography
Model: Julio Chavez
Copyright 2015 © Author Dawn Sullivan
Language: English

Other books by Dawn Sullivan

RARE Series

Book 1 Nico's Heart
Book 2 Phoenix's Fate

White River Wolves Series

Book 1 Josie's Miracle

Dedication

To my Street Team, Dawn's RARE Rebels. Thank you for all that you do. I appreciate all of the time and effort you put into sharing my books on all of the Facebook blogs and to other readers. You all rock!

Also, a special thanks to all of my beta readers-Karrie, Tabitha, Kathy, Charmarie, Jessica and Marie.

~Dawn

RARE: Rescue And Retrieval Extractions

Angel: RARE Alpha, wolf shifter, strong telepathic

Nico: Angel's right hand man, wolf shifter, telepathic, has the ability to see glimpses of the future

Phoenix: Human turned wolf shifter, telepathic, complete badass, loves anything that goes boom

 Rikki: Human, kick ass sniper, touches objects that others have touched and gets visions of the past, present, and sometimes the future

Jaxson: Wolf shifter, telepathic, RARE's technology expert

Trace: Black panther shifter, telepathic, badass sniper

Chapter 1

Peering through the scope of his sniper rifle, Trace Killion silently watched the men guarding the massive estate below. He was camouflaged high up in the branches of a tree approximately 50 yards from the mansion's front gates. The house had 12 bedrooms, 5 bathrooms, 2 living rooms, a large kitchen and a full basement that was aptly called 'The Dungeon'. The Dungeon was filled with several jail cells where men and women were held captive and tortured. Trace would know; he used to oversee what happened in that basement on a daily basis. He'd even been required to take part in the torture sessions on several occasions. There was a tall, black, wrought iron fence surrounding the estate with numerous guards spread out in various positions on the property. It had originally been more, but Trace was gradually picking them off one by one.

As Trace watched, the man he had been stalking for the past three months stepped through the balcony doors of the master bedroom. Trace felt the tension fill his shoulders as he lined up the shot. He was going to rid the world of the bastard standing in his line of sight, Philip Perez…his father.

Trace felt the anger roll through him as he thought of all the reasons he had to kill Perez. For his mother, for his sister, for the chance at a life with his mate.

Trace's mother, Sophia, was a beautiful African American woman. She was tiny with delicate features, long black hair that hung to her waist, beautiful dark brown eyes, and a smile that lit up a room. Sophia had grown up in a large, loving family. She'd been the Cordell princess; doted on by her father, spoiled by her mother, and adored by her two older brothers. Sophia had become a largely sought after cover model at the age of 14. At the age of 15, she caught the eye of Philip Perez, a notorious drug lord and leader of a Colombian drug cartel. When she was just 16 years of age, Philip Perez had broken into her home, killing her parents and brothers and taking a young, terrified Sophia home as his bride. After three months of beating her into submission, Philip had the meek and mild wife he wanted. One year later, after a very hard pregnancy, Trace was born.

Philip Perez had wanted several sons, but Trace's birth had been hard on Sophia's small body. The doctor urged Philip and Sophia not to have any more children. He said Sophia's body could not handle it and it could kill both Sophia and the baby. Philip did not listen, and Sophia had no say in the matter. A year later, she became pregnant again. She lost the baby and almost lost her own life after four months. The doctor had to do an emergency hysterectomy which meant Sophia could no longer have children. Three months later, Philip moved Sophia out of the master bedroom and moved his mistress into the mansion and into his bed. While he lavished his young, coldhearted bitch of a mistress with beautiful clothes and jewelry, Sophia hid in her room. She considered herself blessed when Philip visited her only once or twice a month to take what he considered was his. Those nights were hell. She normally could not get out of bed for days after he beat and raped her.

When Trace was four, his father's mistress became pregnant. Philip was ecstatic. He was finally about to get what he wanted, another son. Nine months later, a baby girl was born. She was so tiny and perfect, with darkly tanned skin and a dark brown tuft of hair on her head. When Philip saw his mistress had given him a daughter instead of a son, he took out his gun and shot her in the head. Taking the baby, he gave her to Sophia and told her to either raise her or kill her, he didn't care which. To him, a female child was useless. Sophia accepted the child into her life, naming her Starr. Sophia used to gaze out the window at night, watching the stars and wishing she was anywhere except with her brutally cruel husband.

After that, Philip turned his entire attention to Trace. Being born into the Colombian drug business,

Trace was groomed from an early age to eventually take over his father's position in the cartel. He was taught not only the ins and outs of the drug business, but how to torture and kill to get what you needed at any cost.

Trace may have been raised to be a killer, but he loved his mother and Starr. For years, Trace watched the pain and abuse his father had bestowed upon them, until finally he was strong enough and had the means to put an end to it. Starr had turned 21 and Trace's dad decided to marry her off to one of his business associates. The man was a known rapist and pedophile, and Trace was not going to allow his little sister to be used and abused by the sick fuck. One night while his father was sleeping, Trace snuck Sophia and Starr out of that same mansion that was sitting in front of him now. He killed any guard that stood in his way. Once they were safely away and Trace was sure they had not been followed, he took his mother and sister to a remote destination and hid them. He vowed that he would keep them safe and would not allow his father to hurt them anymore.

Trace hired two men he trusted to stay with his mother and Starr for protection. Then he moved on to keep his father's attention centered on him and away from his family. He'd been able to save up a large sum of money from the portion of his cuts he received from the drug dealings with his father. However, it was expensive to keep two full time guards and to travel to see his mother and Starr. It was also expensive to travel back to Colombia periodically to keep an eye on his father and make sure he was nowhere near Sophia and Starr. Over the past three years, Trace moved his family every six months to ensure they were never found. He had not saved them from years of mental and physical abuse just to let his father find them and take them back.

With his money supply running low, Trace needed to find a job. After finally getting away from his father and the cartel, he refused to have anything to do with the drug business. Making several subtle inquiries, Trace discovered RARE was looking for a sniper. RARE, Rescue and Retrieval Extractions, was a team of mercenaries who found and rescued victims no one else could. They accepted jobs no one else wanted. Trace needed money to continue hiding his family from Perez, so he tracked down the leader of RARE, Angel Johnston, and asked for a job. He wasn't sure he would make it through the background check, but Angel had gotten back to him within two days to let him know he was hired. Trace knew she had delved deep into his past, but Angel did not ask questions and he didn't volunteer any information. After being hired, Trace found out that every team member of RARE had special abilities. Some were shifters, some not. All were telepathic. Trace hadn't told Angel about his own telepathic ability, but somehow she had known.

As Trace watched, his father stepped to the edge of the balcony, talking on his cell phone. Trace lined up the shot. He was going to take the bastard out now. Just as his finger tightened on the trigger, the sound of a gunshot cracked in the air and Trace felt a sharp pain as a bullet struck his shoulder. Fuck, someone had seen him. Throwing his bag over his shoulder, Trace grabbed his sniper rifle and jumped off the large branch he had been crouched on to the ground several feet below. Taking off at a sprint, he jumped over a log, skirted around a tree and came to a dead stop at the sight before him. Six of his father's men held guns on him, waiting for a reason to fire. Weighing his options, Trace decided the best course of action was to stand down. He needed to live, needed to find a chance to fight back. Today was not the day to die. He had to get home to his mate.

"Drop your gun and bag now," one of the men ordered. "Hands behind your head." Trace slowly lowered his weapon and backpack to the ground, clasping his hands behind his head. The man chuckled cruelly. "Mr. Perez has been waiting for you." Without warning, he slammed his rifle into the gunshot wound on Trace's shoulder. Trace grunted, the pain rolling through him. He refused to show mercy to these men. "Fuck you," he snarled.

Trace knew where he was headed…The Dungeon. He had been there before. Never on the receiving end of the punishment, but that was about to change. To his knowledge, no one had escaped The Dungeon before, unless it was in a body bag. Trace vowed to be the first to not only survive, but to destroy everyone associated with his father. Standing tall, Trace carefully looked each man in the eye. He wanted to make sure he knew who to kill first when he was free. Every last one of the arrogant bastards was going to die.

Strolling casually around Trace, the man who seemed to be in charge laughed again. "Act tough now. Soon you will be crying like a baby. The Dungeon does that to a person. It takes your will to survive. Makes you wish you were dead so you don't have to endure anymore pain." Stopping in front of Trace, the man leaned in close. His black, soulless eyes widened and he rasped, "Soon you will be praying to whatever God you believe in to take your life. When that time comes, make sure and say my name. You pray to Titus. I am your mother fucking God now. Your future lies in my hands." Stepping back with a scowl on his face, the man nodded to someone behind Trace. Pain swamped him and he fell to his knees after the butt of a rifle connected with the side of his head. Struggling to rise, Trace blinked rapidly to get the blood out of his eyes. As his vision blurred, Trace groaned and collapsed on the ground, slowly losing consciousness.

~

Not a lot scared Trace, but waking up naked and chained to the wall in a cell in The Dungeon scared the piss out of him. Struggling to his feet, Trace tested the thick, heavy chains that held him. They were wrapped several times around his chest and down both arms. Even with his shifter strength, there was no way he could break them. He was surprised they had gone to such measures to restrain him, and fear slowly started to seep in that maybe his father knew more about Sophia's side of the family then he had let on in the past. Because Trace's shifting ability did not come from his father.

Peering intently into the darkened room, Trace reacquainted himself with the area. There were a total of 10 cells, similar to jail cells, including the one Trace was in. Only two of the others held hostages. One was a man, and from what Trace could tell, he would not be there much longer. Someone had done a number on him. He lay just inside the closed door of the cell, blood covering his body. He was missing one ear, an arm and who knew what else.

In the other cell directly across from Trace was a woman. She was huddled in the corner with her knees up to her chest, her arms wrapped tightly around her legs. Her long, straggly dark hair covered her face. Trace could sense the terror that filled her. Slowly, as if sensing his eyes on her, the woman raised her head and looked directly at him. Her soft, brown eyes were filled with fear and despair. Tears ran down her dirt covered cheeks. She still wore clothes, unlike Trace and the other unfortunate man in The Dungeon with them, but they were torn and filthy. The woman watched him for a moment longer, and then sighing deeply, she rested her forehead on her knees and started to rock back and forth.

Letting his gaze wander away from the woman, Trace continued casing the room. He wanted to familiarize himself with the area before his captors returned. The table they strapped their prisoners to for interrogation and torture was to the right of his cell. The wall beyond the table was covered with their torture devices. Trace's eyes widened as he took in the number of weapons on the wall. It looked like they had added a number of toys to the mix since he had last been there. Fuck. This was going to hurt. He had no doubt when his father's men came for him, they would use everything they had to try and break him.

Trace stiffened when he heard the door at the top of the stairs open. Bright lights filled the room right before he heard footsteps coming down the stairs. As he watched, the bastard from the jungle appeared at the bottom of the stairs and made his way over to Trace, two men following him. Catching his father's scent, Trace growled, just barely holding back from baring his fangs.

Opening the door to Trace's cell, Titus walked in and stopped in front of him. With a smirk, he chuckled. "Not so tough now, are you?" Slamming his fist into Trace's jaw, Titus laughed again. "You are mine now. I own you." Pulling back an arm, Titus let his fist fly again, filling Trace's mouth with blood. With a snarl, Trace spit the blood into Titus's face.

"Enough," a deep voice ordered as Titus raised his fist again in fury. Trace knew that voice. It was from the nightmares of his past. A voice he would never get out of his head. A voice that had commanded many men to be beat and tortured, many women to be raped and violated. As his son, Trace, had not been exempt from any of it. Not only was Trace on the receiving end of his father's fists many times, but Perez seemed to take pleasure in ordering his men to kick the shit out of Trace on a regular basis. Eventually, Trace had learned not to defy him. Then Trace became the giver of the beatings instead of the receiver. However, one thing Trace had never done was rape another human being. He would have made his father kill him first before being forced to violate another person in that way.

"So, my son has finally come home," Philip Perez said snidely. "Unfortunately, he did not bring with him what he took from me." Entering the cell, his father stood before him, pure hate in his eyes. "I want what you took from me," he growled. "Where are they?"

Trace refused to say a word. There was no way he was giving up his mother and sister. He knew if his father got them back, they would suffer horribly. Trace refused to let that happen. His mother and Starr had been the one constant thing in his life that he could always count on. After the beatings had taken place, they would slip into Trace's room. His mother would tend his wounds while Starr sang softly to him. If his father had found out, both Sophia and Starr would have been punished. But that did not stop them. There was no way Trace was going to allow his father or his father's men near them.

"Fuck you," he growled fiercely. "You might as well kill me now, because I will never tell you where they are."

"Kill you? Oh, I am not going to kill you," Perez sneered. "But by the time I am done with you, you will wish you were dead." Turning to leave, Perez turned back once he reached the bottom of the stairs. "Proceed," he ordered his men before leaving. As the door at the top of the stairs closed, the men unhooked the chains holding Trace to the wall and roughly shoved him towards the table. Trace fought as they wrestled him onto the table, hooking the chains to the four corners.

Hearing a gasp, Trace turned his head to see the woman had risen to her feet and was standing with her hands clenching the bars. No, he would not allow her to be punished because of him. *No.* He pushed the word gently into her mind. *Sit back down.* He ordered. The woman's eyes widened in shock. Slowly she moved back against the wall and sank back down.

Please, Trace heard a female voice in his head. *What can I do to help you?*

There is nothing you can do, he responded, yanking on the chains again. *I will be fine. Just be quiet and don't draw attention to yourself.*

Why are they doing this to us? Why? she asked.

Trace growled, his eyes on the men as they picked their choice of weapon to begin his torture. *You don't know why you are here?*

No, the woman said. *They came in the middle of the night, killing my parents and brother. They took me and my little sister, Sari. They put me down here, but I don't know where Sari is. I haven't seen her since we got here.*

How old is your sister? Trace asked.

Fourteen, the woman responded. Dammit. Trace fought harder against the chains, but there was nothing he could do. He knew why they wanted Sari. He didn't understand why they were keeping the woman down in The Dungeon, but his sick fuck of a father was keeping Sari because he liked young girls. The woman in the cell looked to be in her twenties. The fourteen year old was what Perez preferred.

"You like the woman, do you?" Titus laughed cruelly, as he walked back over to the table. "Maybe I will let you watch later while I take her." Trace stiffened right before Titus struck him with the tire iron on the knee, sending excruciating pain in his knee and up his leg. The beating started then, Trace taking blow after crushing blow. He heard the woman's screams in the background. She was yelling at them, telling them to leave him alone. He did not have the energy to speak to her again and tell her to stop. He just prayed they would not turn their attention to her after they were finished with him.

When the pain was too much, he blocked it out by bringing thoughts of his mate to the surface. His sweet, innocent, beautiful Jade with long blonde locks of hair and dark green eyes. He needed to get back to her. He would withstand whatever pain and agony he had to, so he could return home to his mate.

Before he lost consciousness, he could have sworn he heard Jade's voice, *Trace, where are you?*

~

Jade lurched into a sitting position on the settee where she was resting. Struggling to erase the fog from her mind, she glanced around to get her bearings. She was sitting on her mother, Angel's back porch. Jade was still in shock that she had been reunited with her mother after being kidnapped and held by the General for the past twenty years. She could not believe she was finally away from that bastard. Three months ago, Jade had been rescued by RARE from a prison in Arizona where the General held her. Not only was she reunited with her mother when she was rescued, but she also met her mate, Trace. Closing her eyes, Jade pictured Trace. He was so gorgeous. Several inches taller than her slight frame, he was powerfully built with wide shoulders and a stocky build. He had dark, smooth skin, and was sexy as hell. She shuddered as she remembered his dark eyes that seemed to see into her soul. For the first time, Jade had lost sight of the ultimate goal she and her brother, Jinx, were working toward. For a few hours, the only person Jade had been able to think of was Trace. Until he left her, then the screwed up mess of a life she led seeped quickly back into her consciousness.

Frowning, Jade tried to remember her dream. Or had it been a dream? Had it really been Trace? Was he in trouble? The General had pumped Jade full of so many drugs to keep her gifts dormant that she was having trouble distinguishing what was real and what wasn't. Many of the drugs had been flushed out of her system, but until they were fully gone, there was no way of knowing. Closing her eyes, Jade brought Trace to the forefront of her mind and tried to reach out to him. Finding nothing but emptiness, she sighed deeply. Either her mate was in trouble or her mind was playing tricks on her. Unfortunately, she had no way of knowing which one it was. Rising, she went to find Angel. She had asked her mother several times about Trace, always to be told the same thing. Trace was making it safe for Jade to be with him. He would let Angel know when he was coming back, but he would be back. That did not help Jade now. Not if he was in trouble. But unless she wanted to share her secrets with everyone, she would have to stand down and wait for Trace to return. Since her secrets were not just hers alone, she was forced to stand down. For now, she would just inquire about her mate. But once she had her gifts fully back, she was going hunting. Until then, she would continue to play the sweet, innocent Omega wolf.

Chapter 2

Five months later

      Jade quickly ducked low and scrambled to the left, just barely missing the foot aimed at her face. It glanced off her shoulder in a stunning blow. She should have easily blocked it, but her mind was elsewhere. Jade's mate had left eight months ago and promised to return as soon as he was able to. Not only had Trace not returned, but he had not checked in for over six and a half months. From what Jade knew about mates, they were supposed to love and cherish each other above all else. It was a bonding of souls and it happened fast and hard. Being apart from a mate sucked ass and that was where Jade was right now. Even though she and Trace had not fully bonded yet, Jade was having issues eating and sleeping and her emotions were all over the place. One moment she was crying, and the next she wanted to beat the hell out of something. That was not her. Normally she had tight control over her actions and emotions. She had to; she had secrets to keep and people to protect.

Jade had been taught at a young age to keep a shield in place in her mind, guarding her thoughts and emotions. It was necessary and over time the shield had grown so strong that no one was able to penetrate it. Jade let others see only what she wanted them to see, which was why all of the RARE team members and the White River Wolves assumed she was an Omega wolf. Not only was Jade fine with that assumption, she encouraged it without actually confirming it. Jade was not an Omega wolf. She was so much more.

As Flame struck out again, this time with her fist, Jade decided she'd had enough. She could not keep her mind in the game and needed to be alone. There was no way Flame would stop unless Jade made her, though. Flame had been on a mission for the past seven months. She had been a prisoner of the General's; a sadistic, evil bastard that had started a breeding program to make the ultimate army of soldiers. The General paired men and women with specific physic abilities or shifter traits. Flame was not a shifter, but she had other psychic gifts. She had been paired with Gideon, one of the General's soldiers who raped her repeatedly until she became pregnant. Several months later, during a rescue mission by RARE, Flame lost her unborn son. Even though the baby was conceived under horrible conditions, Flame had learned to love him. Now she made it her life's mission to hunt down not only

Gideon, but also the General and end them. She trained hard, fought hard, and refused to give up.

Grabbing hold of Flame's fist before it could connect with her face, Jade slipped her hands down and held tightly onto Flame's wrists. Dropping down quickly onto her ass, Jade stuck her feet in Flame's stomach and used the power in her legs to flip Flame up and over Jade, landing her on her back. Swinging around, Jade sat on Flame's chest and shoved her elbow up into Flame's larynx. "Stand the fuck down," Jade growled, letting her eyes go wolf and her fangs show. "I'm done."

Flame's eyes widened in shock and she slowly nodded. In all their months of training together, not once did Jade show the type of aggression that was radiating from her now. An Omega wolf would never act forceful or hostile. "Where did you learn that move, Jade?" Flame asked in confusion. "Rikki never taught us that."

Shrugging, Jade stood up and walked to where she had left her coat hanging on the peg by the door. She and Flame were working out daily in the barn on Angel's land. Jade was living with Angel now, so it was a convenient place for her to work out. Not to mention, it was also a dream gym. It was equipped with cardio machines, a couple of punching bags, mats to spar on, and weights. And it was heated, so even in January it was warm. There was also a shooting range set up on the south side of the barn, and Jade was going to go take full advantage of it now. After pulling on her coat, Jade grabbed the gun and box of bullets she had left on the cabinet next to the door. Shoving the bullets into her coat pocket, she glanced back at Flame. "I'm going to shoot for a while. I'll catch you later."

After getting everything set up at the shooting range, Jade loaded her gun. Squinting slightly, arms held out in front of her in the police stance Rikki had taught her, Jade took aim, lining up the shot. Slowly squeezing the trigger, she unloaded the Glock at the paper target several yards away. When she was done, she put the gun down and reeled in the paper. Not bad, Jade thought as she saw the holes in the circles surrounding the bulls-eye. She had hit exactly where she aimed.

"Good job," Rikki said sarcastically as she appeared behind Jade. "Now, tell me why you didn't hit the bulls-eye. After that, you can tell me how you took Flame down the way you did." Shit, she should have known Rikki had been watching them spar. Taking a deep breath, Jade turned to confront Rikki. Resting her hands on her hips she challenged, "I don't know what you mean. I did well. All my shots are in the circles." Eight months ago Jade never would have spoken to anyone the way she was speaking to Rikki. Eight months ago, Jade would have been shoved down in a deep, dark hole with snakes and spiders for daring to say what was on her mind. That was eight months ago, this was now. Before, she was not living. She was surviving. Now, Jade promised herself she would be the person she wanted to be, not what someone else required her to be, as long as she could still keep her deepest secrets. There was no hole to stick her in here and no General to ply her with drugs to dull her senses so she could not fight back. She would never be the helpless woman she was before. She may have to hide her skills and gifts, but she did not have to hide her true personality. Well, not all of the time anyway; only when she felt it beneficial to play the meek, gentle Omega.

Rikki reached out snatching the target. The anger and tension in Rikki rolled off her and Jade cringed at the impressions that hit her fast and hard. Shit, she had let her shield down. Rikki was upset and hurt. It had something to do with a man, a very handsome man. He was tall, dark and muscular with gorgeous brown eyes. He seemed familiar, but the images were rolling by so quickly in her mind, Jade could not grasp who he was. Finally, they slowed down and Jade felt the confusion and despair in Rikki as there was an image of her watching the man being driven away in a SUV, his hand lightly resting on the window.

Turning away from Rikki, Jade calmly squeezed her eyes shut, biting her bottom lip and concentrated on pushing all of the images out of her mind and blocking Rikki's feelings. Damn, it was getting harder and harder to block everything out. Since RARE rescued Jade from the General, she discovered the pills the scientists filled her with had contained something preventing her from fully using her abilities. Jade had not realized how strong those abilities really were. First of all, she was a very strong empath. Constantly feeling others emotions really sucked; the pain, the despair, the jealousy, the anger. There were so many emotions and when you were bombarded with them constantly, it was very hard to block them out and stay sane.

Jade had also known she was telepathic, but thought she was not a very strong one because she was never able to connect with another person unless they held the connection on their end. Now that all of the medicine she had been forced to take was out of her system, Jade was finding out she was not only telepathic, but what she could do went way beyond just talking to someone else with her mind. Jade also had the ability to connect with others like her mother, Angel, could. She found she could easily connect with anyone around her. She tried not to take advantage of her gift, but if her shields were not firmly in place, sometimes it was hard to block others thoughts.

Finally, Jade's head cleared and she was able to push Rikki's thoughts and emotions aside. Calmly, Jade picked up her gun and proceeded to load it.

"Dammit, Jade, stop ignoring me. Get pissed, yell, scream, but don't ignore me." Rikki held the target in front of Jade. "Stop screwing with me, Jade. Stop hiding who you are and what you can do. You are safe now.   The General isn't here. It is just you and me. Hit the fucking target."

Swallowing hard, jaw clenched, Jade watched as Rikki attached a new target to the clamp and reeled it back out. "Now, hit the red," Rikki ordered. "I don't want to see a bullet hole anywhere else on that target, do you understand me? Hit it!"

Looking Rikki in the eyes, Jade took a deep breath. "How did you know?" she asked softly. Not saying a word, Rikki held up a gloved hand, eyebrows raised. Shit. Rikki had the ability to see the past, present and future with the touch of her hand. She wore gloves to prevent the images from constantly bombarding her. Jade wished she had that option. She had to make sure and keep her shields up, or every thought and emotion would hit her.

Nodding, Jade glanced around to make sure no one was around, then she raised her gun and proceeded to unload it hitting the bulls-eye every single time. Turning back to Rikki she asked, "Are you happy now?"

Quickly reeling the target back in and removing it, Rikki grinned. "Now that's what I'm talking about! Why hide it, Jade? Why hide from everyone?"

"Because of Jinx," Jade responded. Placing the gun on the shelf in front of her, she pulled her long blonde hair up in a ponytail securing it with an elastic band she took from around her wrist. Picking up the gun, she proceeded to reload it. "My brother is still with the General. Jinx will do everything in his power to stop him. He taught me how to defend myself. He wanted to make sure I would have a fighting chance if he was able to get me out of there. He could not just take me and run, though. If he did, there wouldn't be anyone to fight the General from the inside. Now that I am with my mother and RARE, Jinx can do what needs to be done on his end without me being a distraction."

"That doesn't make sense to me, Jade." Rikki protested. "There is no reason to hide who you are. You don't need to hide your skills. Jinx can take care of himself. He has for the past 24 years. You need to train harder. You need to push yourself and your abilities, so that when it comes time, you can help Jinx take down the General. Because I promise you, we are all going to help and you are going to want to be there."

"If the General finds out everything I can do, he will hunt me down," Jade insisted. "If he catches me, I will be his prisoner again and Jinx will become his prisoner, too, because the General will know Jinx is the only one that could have trained me in the things that I know. Jinx has done so much for me, Rikki. I can't let him get caught."

"You have been with us for several months, Jade. The General isn't going to think anyone other than RARE trained you," Rikki responded. "Now, we are going to go hand to hand and I want to see what you have. None of this girly bullshit you have been pulling."

"Jinx taught me to fight, Rikki. I have his fighting style. Not many do. The General will know." Jade hesitated, as she watched Angel, Nico, Phoenix, Jaxson and Ryker coming toward them. They were all training together today, but Jade and Flame had decided to practice together before the others arrived. Now they were close enough to hear Jade and Rikki's argument. Jade was pissed. How dare Rikki put Jinx in danger? Who the hell did she think she was? Jinx had been there for Jade since they had met 20 years ago. No one else had been there. Not Angel, not her father, just Jinx. And no one would put his life at risk if Jade could help it. Jinx was in enough danger as it was.

"Let's do this, Jade. Now!" Rikki ground out, jabbing at Jade quickly with her fist. Jade easily blocked it. Laughing, Rikki kicked out with her foot, jabbing Jade in the thigh hard and then jumping back.

"Is that it? All you can do is block? You aren't going to save your brother and take down the General with those moves. Of course, if that is all Jinx taught you, then maybe he will be dead before we can save him anyway."

Jade saw red. Fuck Rikki. No one was going to get to her brother. In the background, she heard Angel ordering Rikki to stand down, but Jade could not stop herself. Rikki had pushed too hard. Leaping forward, Jade slammed an elbow into Rikki's mouth, then quickly swept Rikki's feet out from under her. Rikki landed on her ass but swiftly rolled out of the way and was up and ready to go.

"Both of you stand down now!" Angel ordered as she stopped in front of them. "I don't know what's going on here, but you need to back away from each other."

Jade moved in close to Rikki, her hands tightly balled into fists at her side, her body shaking with fury. "Stop hiding," Rikki snarled. "Show us who you really are."

Grabbing Rikki by the throat, Jade slammed her up against the barn. Growling low, Jade threatened, "If anything happens to my brother because of you, I will kill you." The sight of the blood trailing down Rikki's chin along with the brief glimpse of fear in Rikki's eyes finally broke through the haze in Jade's mind. Quickly stepping back, Jade fought to raise her shields and find that inner peace that would make all of her pain and suffering fade once again into the background. Breathing deeply and fighting for that inner calm, Jade slowly backed away from the stunned team. "I need to get away for a while," she whispered brokenly. "I need to be alone. I'm going for a run."

Angel nodded silently. "Rikki," she said after a moment, "we were just coming to get you. Jeremiah called and we are needed on a mission." Turning to her team she told them, "You are on your own this time. Nico, you are in charge. I trust you to get the job done. I'm staying here with my daughter. She needs me."

"No," Jade interrupted Angel. "I need to be alone. I'm sorry, I need time to myself. Go with your team." When Angel looked like she was going to argue, Jade insisted, "You saw what just happened, Angel. I'm not ready to talk about it, but if I don't get some time alone someone might get hurt." Sighing deeply, Jade fought the tears that threatened to break free. "If I need anything, I will call Chase. He will send someone."

Chase was the Alpha of the White River wolf pack that lived near Boulder, Colorado. He was Angel's mate, even though both seemed to be fighting the mate bond. He was also raising two little girls

RARE had rescued from the same facility where Flame was held. Two little girls Angel wanted to claim as her own, but was unable to. Jade was not sure what was going on between Chase and Angel, but there were several times she had used her abilities to try to calm both when they were together. Jade had the ability to affect emotions occasionally, but it didn't always work. Chase and Angel were proof of that.

"I don't like the thought of you alone, Jade," Angel argued. "What if the General sends his men after you while I'm gone? I won't be here to protect you. Neither will RARE. I need all of them on this mission."

"Then you obviously need to go, too," Jade retorted. "I will be fine. You haven't been on a mission in the eight months I have been here. Just go. If I need anything, Jinx…" Jade trailed off realizing what she had been about to say. She did not want anyone to know how close Jinx was right now. It wasn't safe.

Understanding dawned in Angel's gaze. Tears filled her eyes. "He's near, isn't he, Jade?" she questioned. "You have been secretly meeting with him. My son is near and wants nothing to do with me." Back stiffening, her voice hard, Angel turned to her team. "Get ready to head out. We leave in 15 minutes." Seeing Flame standing by the barn door,

Angel ordered, "You will stay with my daughter, Flame. Maybe she and her brother will tolerate your presence better than mine." Not waiting for a response, Angel headed back to the house without looking back.

Jade felt the angry gazes of the team members, but refused to look any of them in the eye. They could think what they wanted. Right now, keeping Jinx safe was all that mattered. She would fight to the death for her brother.

Chapter 3

It was dark, so dark and cold. Waves of fear poured off Jade as she tried to remember where she was. The hole. She had to be back in the hole. She was sitting on the hard, cold ground, her back up against a wall. Tentatively, she moved her hand across the wall behind her and flinched when she felt cold cement scrape her fingertips. Cement, not dirt. She was definitely not in the hole.

When she tried to move her hand further, she was stopped. That was when Jade realized she was bound in chains. They were wrapped around her arms several times and hooked to the wall behind her. They were also wrapped around the upper part of her body and were digging into her chest so tight she could barely breathe. She yanked on them again and again, but could not get loose. As her fear escalated into full-on terror, she heard a door open and a dim light flickered on. Squinting through swollen eyes, Jade watched as a man approached her. Again and again, she yanked on the chains, but she was going nowhere. She was tightly secured.

The man squatted down in front of Jade. His dark, savage eyes stared into hers. "You thought you were going to get free, didn't you? Have you started praying to your god yet?" he rasped viciously to her. "Remember, I am your god. I decide your future. You beg to me. You pray to me…Titus." Rising back up to his full height, Titus walked over to a table on the far side of the room. Walking behind it, he removed a hammer from the wall and walked back toward her, lightly tapping the hammer in the palm of his hand. "You have lasted longer in The Dungeon than I thought you would; longer than anyone before you. I would have killed you by now, but you have information the boss wants."

What the hell was he talking about? She had never seen this man before. Where was she? Did the General have her again? Looking around, her eyes widened as she caught a glimpse of several jail cells lined up along the walls around the room. Some contained people, some were empty. The people in them looked half dead, which did not surprise her the way she was feeling right now.

The door opened again and two more men walked in. Walking over to the wall, one removed a steel baseball bat, the other a tire iron. Oh God, she thought as they stepped in her direction. The first man laughed as he unhooked one of the chains holding her to the wall. "Are you ready for round two?"

"Leave him alone, you fucking animals!" Jade heard a woman scream. Weakly raising her head, she stared across the room at a woman who seemed to be reaching for her through the bars of her cell. Her long, ratty, dark hair hung in dirty, greasy clumps around her face. Her clothes were filthy and were hanging on her small, thin frame. Her face was swollen and bruised, one arm hung limply at her side.

Jade fought to get free as the men drug her to the table, lifting her onto it and chaining her down. Slowly, she felt the fight drain out of her and she turned her head to where the woman stood sobbing, her hand tightly clenching the bar to her cell. "Please, fight Trace. You have to fight," the woman begged. *Trace?* Jade thought, trying to wade through her sluggish mind. Her eyes widened as she suddenly realized what was happening.

No, she screamed in her mind, *no!* The man raised the hammer and brought it down swiftly, but right before it connected with her flesh, she had the strange feeling that someone pushed her away…then there was complete darkness.

Jade sat up in bed, a silent scream on her lips. A dream…it was only a dream. But it seemed so real. She was shaking from pure terror. Jade kept replaying over and over in her mind the psychotic look in the man's eyes as he swung the hammer toward her. It had seemed so real. Obviously it wasn't. She was fine, safe at home in her bed.

It was not a memory. Jade had never been in a place like that before. There was no way she would forget it. The jail cells, the torture devices on the wall by the table on the side of the room, the deranged lunatic coming after her with a hammer. But she could not get over how real it felt.

Jade's eyes widened in comprehension as she remembered the strange feeling of being pushed away from the horrific things that were about to take place. That was because it had not been either a memory or a dream. It was real, and someone was going through it right now. She had somehow connected with someone who was in the process of being tortured. "Trace," she whispered. It had to be Trace. Closing her eyes, she remembered the woman screaming his name.

God, she hadn't heard from Trace in months. She was his mate. He would have called. He would have checked in if he was able to. For the first month and a half he was gone, Trace had made contact at least once a week, if not twice. If he could, Trace would have still been calling. Jade knew in her gut that the person being tortured was her mate. Moaning softly, she fought the fear that threatened to consume her. Trace was in pain. He was in so much pain.

Squeezing her eyes shut, Jade tried to connect with Trace again. She did anything and everything she could think of, but it was no use. He had locked her tightly out, probably thinking to keep her safe. Jade was strong, but not strong enough to penetrate Trace's walls, especially not with the distance between them. She needed help. Unfortunately, Angel and the team were on a mission. When they went out on an op, they went radio silent until the job was done. She could try and connect telepathically with Angel, but if they were in the middle of a rescue attempt, it would not be smart to distract her.

Jade had to find Trace. She had to save him. Jumping out of bed, she screamed for Flame who was sleeping in the room next to hers. Yanking open her dresser drawer, Jade pulled out a pair of camo pants and a long sleeved, black shirt, quickly pulling them on. Bursting through the door, gun in hand, Flame quickly looked around for an enemy.

"There is no one here," Jade said as she sat down on the bed to put on a pair of socks and her boots. "We have to go. Trace is in trouble. We need to get to him."

"Trace?" Flame asked in confusion. "Where is he? Did he call?" Slowly, Flame lowered her gun and wiped her bleary eyes. She had obviously been woken from a deep sleep and was having trouble keeping up.

"No," Jade said as she hurriedly pulled on her boots. "I connected to him in a dream. They are hurting him, Flame. We need to go now. I need to get to him."

"Go where?" Flame demanded. "Where is he? Who has him?" Jade froze. Shit, she didn't know. She didn't have the answers to that question. All she knew for sure was that somebody had her mate and, was at that very moment torturing him. How could she find him? She had tried to reconnect with him, but he had blocked her out. Jade knew that he was not near. She knew he was thousands of miles away, in another country. Unfortunately, she had no idea what country. Neither Trace nor Angel had told her what was going on. All she knew was Trace was trying to make it safe for them to be together. Out of respect for Trace and Angel, Jade had never tried to connect with either of them to find out the truth.

Looking up at Flame, feeling lost and scared, Jade whispered, "I don't know, Flame. I have no idea where he is. I don't know how to find him. I tried to connect to him again, but he blocked me out."

Flame studied her for a moment, lost in thought. "What about Jinx?" she asked. "He's very strong. He connected with Serenity when you were attacked by that rogue wolf months ago and helped her save your life. If he can do something like that, maybe he can somehow help find Trace."

"No," Jade protested shaking her head adamantly. "No, I can't ask Jinx to help. He is in too much danger as it is. I won't pull him into more. If the General suspects Jinx has anything to do with me, he will demand Jinx hunt me down and bring me back. When Jinx refuses, because he will, the General will have him killed. I can't involve him in this."

"So you will let your mate die instead?" Flame asked. Sitting down beside Jade, Flame tentatively put her arm around Jade's shoulder. "I'm not asking you to choose between your mate and your brother, Jade. I am asking you to give your brother the option to help you, and to give your mate a fighting chance."

Jade roughly pushed a hand through her long blonde hair, her dark green eyes bright with tears she fought to hold back. "Trace needs me," she whispered. "There is no one else that can help him."

Swallowing hard, Jade made her decision. Picturing Jinx in her mind, she called to him. *I need you my brother. Please, I need your help.* She did not have to wait long. Jade felt Jinx's presence in her mind almost instantly. The twins had connected so many times in the past it was almost second nature to them now.

I'm here, Jinx responded. Just the sound of her brother's voice calmed her. Jinx had always been there for her. Sometimes when the General stuck her down in the hole, Jade and Jinx would talk for hours. Jinx loved to read, and he would share his love of books with Jade. Sometimes he would even read to her. Other times they talked about their lives; past, present, and hopes and dreams for the future. They shared things with each other that they would never share with anyone else. Jade trusted Jinx, and only Jinx. Trust was something that had to be earned; Jinx was the only person in Jade's life who had earned her trust. She was getting there with Angel, but still had a long ways to go.

Are you near? Jade asked, praying he was. Jinx had shown up two days ago and paid her a surprise visit. They had sat out in the barn and talked until the early hours of the morning. It was the first time she'd heard from him since the incident with the rogue wolf. Jinx was trying to keep his distance so that he did not inadvertently lead the General and his men to Jade. Now that she was free, there was no way he would allow the General to find her again. Jade felt guilty that she kept his visit a secret from Angel, but Jinx was not ready to talk to their mother yet.

The General had been manipulating the lives of Angel, Jinx and Jade from the very beginning. He had originally wanted Angel in his breeding program, but after watching her for several months, he realized acquiring her would be nearly impossible. So he did the next best thing. The General sent one of his most trusted soldiers to Angel with orders to manipulate her into falling for him and giving him a child. The soldier followed orders perfectly and within three months Angel was pregnant with twins. When Jinx and Jade were born, the doctors told Angel that Jinx was stillborn. Angel had been so devastated at the news, she had not questioned the doctors. The General stole Jinx from Angel, and four years later he took Jade.

No, Jinx replied evasively. Jade caught the impression of an older man with smoky grey eyes and dark hair, silver at the temples. He was dressed in a black tux and talking to a younger woman with long blonde hair and bright blue eyes, wearing a deep blood-red colored dress. The woman definitely stood out. It looked like they were at a party, both held wine glasses and the sound of music was in the background.

What are you doing, Jinx? Where are you? Jade asked in confusion. There was no way her brother would be at a lavish party like this by his own free will. Although Jinx was a chameleon and could fit in almost anywhere, he would never choose to be around what he considered the snobbish elite. There was only one reason Jade could think of that Jinx would step foot in that place.

Stalking, was Jinx's short response, confirming Jade's suspicions. The General had sent him. Which meant there was no way she was going to get Jinx's help right now. Even if he wanted to, he could not abort a mission the General sent him on.

Which one, Jade asked after a moment. Once again she got the faint impression of the male. Now he had moved on to talk to a man in a dark navy tux. Before she could see anything else, Jinx blocked the vision. *What the hell, Jinx?* she growled. They never hid anything from each other. They were twins. They had a connection only twins could have. To have Jinx shut her off like that hurt.

This is nothing for you to worry about, Jade. Talk to me. What did you need? Jade growled softly, gritting her teeth in frustration. Having Jinx shut her out pissed her off, but she had more important things to worry about. She had a mate to track down.

Trace is in trouble, she whispered through their connection. *I connected with him somehow, Jinx. He's in so much pain. They are hurting him. But he must have realized I was with him because he shut me out just before a new torture session started. I tried and tried to reconnect with him so that I can track him, but I can't. I'm just not strong enough.*

Jinx was silent for a few minutes. He had shut her out and she could not see what he was doing, but she knew he was in full predator mode. She did not even know why she had told him about Trace. He was on a mission and wouldn't be able to help. But she needed him. Jade knew she couldn't find Trace on her own and Angel wasn't there to help. A tear slipped down her cheek as she realized she was screwed. Her mate was out there suffering, and there was no way she was going to be able to help him right now.

Her eyes snapping open, Jade jumped off the bed and turned, slamming her fist into the wall. Screaming in rage, she hit it again and again. Flame grabbed Jade from behind, wrapping her arms tightly around her. "Shhh, Jade," Flame whispered as she fought to hold her still. "We will find him. I promise you, we will find him."

Jade slowly collapsed on the floor, her body racked with sobs. Flame sat with her and held her, crooning softly. "As soon as Angel gets back from her mission, we will find him, Jade. That is what RARE does. They find and rescue people. I sent her a text already letting her know you need her. She will come as soon as she gets it."

Looking up at Flame, her dark green eyes bright with tears, Jade whispered, "But can Trace wait that long? You weren't there, Flame. He is bound in chains. He can't move, can't fight back. And his pain is overwhelming."

"He will fight to stay alive, Jade. He will fight to survive so he can come back to you," Flame vowed. "It's what mates do."

Allowing herself to do something she hadn't done with anyone but Jinx in years, Jade slowly settled into Flame's arms and accepted her comfort as Flame rocked back and forth. Closing her eyes, her body shuddered as she fought to calm herself. She knew she wasn't helping anyone in this condition.

I will be there tomorrow, she heard Jinx promise right before their link was severed. Just like her brother, short on words but big on action. Sighing, Jade pulled out of Flame's arms and rose to her feet. Shoving her hands through her long, blonde hair, she took a deep breath and said, "Jinx is coming tomorrow. I need to pack. Once we find out where Trace is, I need to leave."

Nodding, Flame stood and walked to the door. Looking back she told Jade, "I will be ready." When Jade would have protested, Flame held up a hand. "Stop. You are not in this alone, Jade. I consider you a friend, and I don't have many of them. I am going with you, whether you want me to or not." Without another word, Flame was gone.

Deciding now was not the time to argue, Jade grabbed a backpack from the closet and placed some clothes in it, along with a few other things she thought she might need. After she was packed, she slung her bag over her shoulder and headed for the kitchen. It was only midnight, but she knew there was no way in hell she would be sleeping again. After storing her bag in a corner, Jade started a pot of coffee, then started to open the door to the basement. Hearing a noise behind her, Jade swung around to meet Flame's gaze. "Let's do this," Flame demanded, as she reached for the door and pulled it all of the way open. Swallowing hard, Jade nodded and made her way down the stairs and to the weapons room. She'd never had anyone have her back before except for Jinx. But to free Trace, she was going to have to start putting her trust in others. She was going to need the help.

Using the keypad on the wall, she entered the code Angel had given her months before to unlock the door. Pausing in the doorway, Jade took a deep breath. There was no going back now. She would do this, for her mate. She would let her true self show, and fuck anyone that got in her way. Resolved, she pushed open the door and entered the room. Grabbing a bag off a shelf, Jade started filling it with explosives, extra bullets, and anything else she thought they would need. When it was full, she grabbed a Glock and stuck it in the back of her pants after verifying the safety was on. After securing a 9mm at her ankle, she slipped a knife into a sheath on her hip and some throwing stars into the pockets on her camo pants. Glancing at Flame, Jade saw that she was geared up and ready to go, too. Grabbing the bag, Jade made her way out of the weapons room and back up the stairs to start the long wait for Jinx. She prayed he was able to complete his current mission before coming to her so he would not have to suffer the General's wrath, but secretly she was just glad he was coming. Jade was ready to find her mate and kick some ass, but she would need her brother to do so.

~

Jinx resisted the urge to yank on the tie that came with the monkey suit he was required to wear so he could easily blend in with the high class crowd surrounding him. He hated snobs, hated crowds of any kind, and wanted to be anywhere but where he was at the moment. And he would be…soon. His sister needed him.

Picking up a flute of champagne from a passing waitress, Jinx wandered closer to his target. The General had sent him to dispense of a senator whom he claimed was blocking movement in the General's breeding program. The truth was, the man was an investor in the program and had threatened to pull his funds if the General didn't help him smuggle under aged girls into the United States from other countries. The girls were being kidnapped and when they reached the states, they were sold at an auction to the highest bidder.

While the General didn't care what happened to those girls, he was pissed the Senator had the nerve to give him an ultimatum. So, he decided he didn't need him around anymore. He would find another investor.

After taking a trip through the Senator's mind, Jinx didn't give a shit about either of the men's motives. The sick fuck raped girls that couldn't be more than 13 or 14, and he was going to die.

When Jinx was within ten feet of the bastard, he stopped and waited for the man to look over. When he did, Jinx smirked. *This is for all of the defenseless little girls you defiled,* he growled softly into the Senator's mind. *You will never hurt any of them again.* Jinx's sardonic grin grew as the Senator started to choke. Dropping the glass he held, the man clawed at his throat with his hands, his eyes begging Jinx to stop. *Just think about how those young girls felt every time you took them,* Jinx snarled, the grin never leaving his face. *Let that be the last thing in your mind when you die, you bastard. This is for them.* The man's eyes widened as he gasped for breath before slowly sliding to the floor as he took his last breath.

Turning, Jinx made his way to the exit, stopping to glance back one last time at the still body of the man lying on the ballroom floor. He had no problem killing if it was justified. And that fucker's death was definitely justified.

Turning, Jinx left the building and handed the valet out front the ticket for his car. He would swap it for a different form of transportation when he left town. He would need something a lot faster than the Cadillac he was driving if he was going to reach Denver in the afternoon.

Chapter 4

Shaking his head to try and clear his vision, Trace struggled uselessly against the chains that held him captive. How the hell did he allow himself to get caught and thrown in The Dungeon? He remembered mistakenly thinking if he went with the bastards who caught him, he would eventually break free and beat feet back to Denver. After killing his father, of course. He should have known better.

Trace groaned as he tried to block out the pain that ravaged his body. His captors visited him at least four times a week to beat the hell out of him and to try and extract information. Trace didn't care what they did; there was no way he was giving up his mother and Starr's location. They would have to kill him.

Leaning back against the concrete wall, Trace let himself relax as he closed his eyes and thought of his one regret, not claiming his mate. Jade...his beautiful, sweet Jade. He'd thought of her numerous times since his captivity and wanted nothing more than to hold her in his arms one more time before he died. She was so beautiful with her long, silky blonde hair, dark green eyes, and soft, milky white skin. So delicate and pure. After everything Trace had done in his past, he knew he didn't deserve someone like

Jade. But fate seemed to think differently. Fate had given him Jade and all he wanted was the chance to love and cherish her. Trace clenched his fists tightly as he imagined Jade going on without him, finding another mate, having children and living happily ever after. Fuck that. Jade was his.

With a loud roar, Trace started to struggle against the chains again, his hands shifting to claws as his panther tried to get out. Jade was his, dammit. His! He wasn't going to give up and die in this fucking hellhole. He was going to escape. He was going to get free and go home to his mate. Then he was going to come back and kill Philip Perez and every motherfucker associated with him.

"Stop, Trace," he heard a weak voice say from the cell next to his. "You have to stop. Conserve your strength. You aren't going to get out of those chains. You have tried so many times."

Snarling, his eyes going cat and his fangs punching through his gums, Trace hissed, "I have to, Gypsy. I have to get home to her."

Her eyes full of sympathy, Gypsy whispered, "And you will, my friend. But you have to calm down. You can't let them see you like this. They can't know your secrets."

Realizing he was out of control, Trace bowed his head and grabbing onto the chains on the wall, he squeezed them tightly. Taking deep breaths to slow his pounding heart, he forced his claws and fangs to recede. Gypsy was right. He needed to gain control over himself and conserve his strength. Hell, he could hardly stand up after the last beat down he was given. Blood flowed freely down his arms and legs. Titus was a master at torture. He knew exactly how much a person could handle before he couldn't go on anymore. And somehow he seemed to know that Trace could handle way more. Trace didn't know if they knew he was a shifter, and he wasn't going to ask. But the signs pointed in that direction. Sighing, he decided he better dig deep for his balls and find a way out. All he needed was one screw up from the people who held him, and he would be free. He was getting the hell out and taking Gypsy and Sari with him.

When he was finally able to look at Gypsy through his own eyes and not the eyes of his cat, he raised his head and peered at her. She was leaning up against the wall in the corner closest to him. Her legs were straight out in front of her and she was cradling her broken arm. The whole left side of her face was swollen and bruised, and there was fresh blood streaming down her temple and neck. "Dammit, Gypsy," he growled. "I told you not to say anything the next time they took me. If you would stop drawing attention to yourself they would leave you alone."

Over the past few months, Trace and Gypsy had become close friends. He had shared things with her that he hadn't even shared with RARE, people he considered his family. She had been moved to the cell near his when their captors brought in more prisoners. They needed the hooks on the wall in her old cell to chain up another man. Since Gypsy was just a woman and they did not see her as a threat, they put her next to Trace in a cell that didn't have hooks to attach chains to. She was fed every three days or so, and was now extremely underweight and malnourished. Trace was lucky if he received food once a week. Once, Gypsy had tried to share her food with him. She'd reached through the bars of her cell, but he was chained too far away. When trying to get the food to him, she accidentally dropped it on the ground. Trace was unable to hide it, and when Titus found out he ordered his men to beat both of them. After that, Trace refused the food she offered him.

No one had come for Gypsy in the five months he had been there. Titus threatened her that first day, but he never did touch her, unless it was to beat her. Trace knew his father kept Gypsy alive so her sister, Sari, would cooperate. He brought Sari to The Dungeon to see her sister once a week. Each time, he allowed Sari in the cell with Gypsy for five minutes. If she didn't leave when the five minutes were up, he would drag her out by her long blonde hair. The first time Sari was allowed to visit Gypsy, she made the mistake of protesting her sister's treatment. Perez made her watch as his men punished Gypsy for Sari's disobedience. He told Sari that he kept Gypsy around as a gift to her, but if Sari made the mistake of saying another word in Gypsy's defense, he would have Gypsy killed. Sari had paled and quickly ducked her head in deference to him and promised to behave. If he were free, Trace would have slit Perez's throat right then and there.

Trace frowned as a thought tickled the back of his mind. God his head hurt. One of the bastards had hit him with something on the back of his head while the others were taking him off the table to return him to his cell. Squeezing his eyes shut and fighting to block the pain out, Trace tried to remember what he knew was important. Feeling the bite of the chains that he still clasped in his hands, he slowly released them allowing himself to fall to the floor. The chains were now just long enough that he could sit down and rest. Leaning his aching head back against the wall, he once again closed his eyes and tried to remember. Fear…terror. There was a presence in his mind. Jade. Somehow Jade had connected with him when he was being taken to the table to be tortured. She had been with him right up until he had shoved her out, refusing to let her be a part of the hell he was about to experience. He had no idea where he came up with the strength to push her away. Trace tried numerous times to connect with Angel after he was unable to escape in the first month. But he was so weak and kept in constant pain. No matter how much he tried, he couldn't find Angel. How the hell had Jade connected with him though? Last he knew, her telepathic ability was almost nonexistent.

Bringing Jade's face up in his mind, he slowly tried to reach out to her. After a few minutes of excruciating pain pounding through his temples, he finally gave up. After working so hard to block her out, it was frustrating as hell that he couldn't reach her now.

"What are you doing?" Gypsy asked softly. Opening his eyes, he cautiously moved his head to glance her way. "I was trying to connect with Jade," he admitted grimly. "I wasn't able to."

"Get some sleep," Gypsy ordered softly. "You need to rest. There is no way you are going anywhere in the shape you're in. I will wake you if they come back."

Sighing, Trace gave in. Gypsy was right. He was of no use to anyone right now. Closing his eyes he allowed himself to slip into a deep sleep. He would try again to connect with his mate when he awoke. His last thought as he slowly lost consciousness was about his mother and sister. He wasn't around to move them like he normally did. He prayed they weren't found before he could get to them.

Chapter 5

Jade sprang to her feet at the sound of the vehicle pulling up in front of the house. Running through the back porch and out the door with Flame on her heels, she froze when she saw Angel and the rest of her team pull up in the black SUV. A tear escaped before she could stop it. It was 5 p.m. and Jinx wasn't there yet, but Angel was. She had come home.

Holding her head high, hands on her hips, Jade waited for Angel to come to her. She was done hiding. What they saw was what they got. Fuck the Omega routine.

Angel stopped about five feet away and took in the sight of Jade and Flame in full mercenary gear. Not batting an eye, she ordered, "Talk to me."

"Trace is in trouble," Jade informed her, a small catch in her throat. Clearing her throat, she straightened her spine and continued, "He is wrapped tightly in thick chains and can't escape." Clenching her jaw, she took a deep breath and made herself continue. "He is being tortured and is in so much pain."

"And you know this how?" Angel demanded roughly as she took another step in Jade's direction, anger in her voice. "Did someone contact you?"

Looking her mother in the eyes, Jade told her, "I connected with him while I was sleeping. I can merge with people just like you can. I am a strong telepath. I honestly didn't realize how strong until all of the drugs the General gave me were out of my system, but I have always known I was stronger than I let on."

Ignoring the fact that her own daughter had been lying to her, Angel asked, "Did he give you his location? He has to be in Colombia, but do you know where?"

Shaking her head, Jade whispered, "No, he shoved me out when he realized I was there. They were starting to torture him and...I guess he was trying to protect me."

"I sent you a text as soon as Jade told me what happened," Flame interjected stepping up beside Jade. "She tried to reconnect with him, but he blocked her out."

"He didn't want you to endure the pain he was going through," Rikki stated. "Even though you weren't the one actually being tortured, chances are high you would have felt all the pain he felt."

Swallowing hard, Jade nodded. "That's what I figured. I would have stayed with him if he would have let me, though. He wouldn't have had to go through it alone."

Pride shining in her eyes at her daughter's words, Angel smiled gently, "I know you would have, Jade." Turning to her team, Angel ordered. "Let's go inside. I'm going to try and connect with Trace. Let's bring our boy home."

As they moved toward the house, the faint sound of a motorcycle could be heard in the distance. Jade whispered, "Jinx," as a dark black Harley with flames on the side turned down Angel's long driveway. Jade waited until he parked the bike in front of the barn, and then with a soft cry, she was off the porch and running to him. Swinging a leg over the bike, Jinx opened his arms and caught his sister as she hurled herself at him. Holding her close, he gently ran a hand down her head. Finally, leaning back he said, "Let's find your mate, sis."

Smiling tremulously, Jade nodded and pulled him to where everyone waited. Angel stood at the top of the stairs drinking in the sight of her son. Dark hair, hard dark brown eyes, black cargo pants with various pockets to hide weapons, and a heavy, black leather coat. The hilt of his sword was just visible from the scabbard on his back. Jade watched as Jinx and Angel eyed each other. Finally, Angel turned and walked into the house with the team following. "We are going to a room in the basement where we talk strategies," Jade told Jinx. "Angel is going to try to reach Trace." Knowing his dislike for enclosed places she offered, "You can wait out here for now."

Shaking his head, Jinx walked up the stairs and into the house, following the rest of the team. While the rest of the team claimed seats around the table, Jinx chose to stay by the open doorway, leaning against the doorjamb. Jade took a seat by Angel and waited to see what would happen. She had never actually taken part in a mission discussion before, and that was exactly what this was. It was a search and rescue mission for Trace.

"I am going to try and connect with Trace first," Angel told them. "I know he was hunting his father in Colombia. Jaxson, pull up everything you can on a drug lord that goes by Philip Perez. He is who we need to find if we want to find Trace."

Jade's eyes widened at the news, but she kept quiet. She needed to let RARE do their magic and right now that meant no interruptions from her unless she had something helpful to add. Nico and Phoenix rose and went to flank Angel. Jade watched Angel close her eyes and grasp the arms of her chair tightly. Breathing slowly in and out, Angel sat for several minutes without moving. Finally, she sighed leaning back in defeat. "I can't reach him," she confessed. "He might be blocking me, too."

"No, he isn't," Jinx said from his spot by the door. "He's unconscious." As everyone looked at him in surprise, he shrugged. "I piggybacked on your thread and kept going when you came up short. He's in a lot of pain, but is unconscious at the moment."

Moving away from the doorjamb, Jinx said, "I'm heading to Colombia now. We know that's where he is. We can connect with him when he's awake to find out more information."

"Jinx, wait," Angel ordered as he started to leave the room. Stopping, but not turning around, Jinx waited for Angel to continue. "We have a plane that can be ready by the time we get to the airport. Ride with us. Please."

Nodding once, Jinx told her, "I will be outside when you are ready." Without another look, he was gone.

Jade reached out and gently clasped Angel's hand. "Jinx has been through hell and back," she whispered. "I will never betray his confidence by giving details, but just know this. He cannot be in small spaces for more than a short period of time. He will go crazy. He prefers the outdoors. He is also very powerful. If he says Trace is unconscious, then it's the truth. Trust his judgment. I do."

Squeezing Jade's hand once before letting go, Angel started handing out orders. "Nico, call and make sure the plane is refueled and waiting for us. Jaxson, I want you to pull up all the information you can on Perez during the flight, so Nico will be piloting with Phoenix this time. Ryker, I know you are in a hurry to get back to your new mate, but I need everyone on this."

"Josie will understand, boss," Ryker said. "Trace is one of ours. We are bringing him home."

"I'm going, too," Storm said from the doorway. Storm was almost killed just the month before when she and Ryker were sent on a mission to hunt down a rogue wolf pack. But she'd worked hard at her physical therapy and after finally being able to shift into her wolf form two weeks ago, she'd begun to heal quickly.

"If Doc Josie clears it, you go," Angel responded. "Ryker, when you call the Doc to let her know you won't be back yet, verify that Storm is cleared for duty."

"I will be outside with Jinx," Jade said when Angel was finished giving out orders. "We will be ready to go when you are." Ignoring the surprised looks of everyone in the room, Jade walked out and took the stairs two at a time. Grabbing her bag on the way through the kitchen, she went out to wait with

Jinx. She was done sitting on the sidelines and playing with the damn babies. She had more training than anyone in that room realized, and she was about to show them all what she could do.

Walking over to Jinx, Jade leaned back against the barn beside him. "How did your mission go?" she asked softly, scanning the perimeter for enemies the way Jinx had taught her.

Nodding approvingly, Jinx responded shortly, "The mission is complete."

"And the General?" Jade pressed. "What will he say when you don't return right away?"

"Nothing," Jinx replied. "I contacted him as soon as it was done and told him I would return after I got laid. He thinks it helps feed my gifts. Dumbass."

Despite the situation, Jade had to laugh. "Really? He thinks having sex gives you more power?"

Shrugging nonchalantly, Jinx told her, "That's what I told him a long time ago. He won't question it unless I am away longer than a couple of days. Besides, as long as I go back and kill the next person on his list, he won't give a shit."

Seeing the pain Jinx tried to hide from her, Jade lightly touched his arm. "It will all be over soon, Jinx. And you haven't killed anyone that didn't deserve to die."

Covering her hand with one of his, Jinx stared out over the farmland surrounding them. "I kill to survive, Jade. I don't want to do it, I sure as hell don't enjoy it, but I have no choice. And I will keep doing it until I shut that bastard down."

Laying her head gently on his shoulder, Jade stood in silence while they waited for Angel and her team. She would give anything to get her brother away from the General. Jinx could kill the General now, but there would be another mad man in the wings waiting to take his place. You had to cut off the tentacles of the monster, not just kill the monster. The General had several people invested in his breeding program, and they could not all be eliminated at once.

Raising her head as Angel walked out of the house, Jade decided to forget about the General and his psychotic schemes for now. She had more important things to worry about. Like her mate.

Chapter 6

Trace groaned as he slowly woke from a deep sleep. Shit, his head hurt. Frowning, he tried to figure out what had awoken him. Gypsy slept fitfully on the hard ground in the cell next to his. There were soft moans of pain coming from a couple of the other cells, but everything else was quiet. Letting his eyes slowly close again, he suddenly stiffened. There was another presence in his mind. The only two people that ever merged with him like this were Angel, and most recently, Jade. This was a male, a very powerful male if he had made it past Trace's shields. Not recognizing him, Trace tried to push him back out, but after the last torture session, he was too weak.

Stop, the man ordered. *You can't get rid of me, so stop your sorry ass attempt.*

Breathing heavily, Trace snarled, *Who the hell are you? What do you want?*

Jinx, the man responded. *Jade's brother. She sent me to track you.*

Jinx, Trace thought. He'd never heard of Jinx. But then, Angel hadn't told them about her daughter, so maybe she'd neglected to tell them about her son, too. Not willing to fully trust someone he didn't know, Trace growled, *So, you found me. Now get the fuck out of my head.*

You are just as stubborn as my sister, Jinx retorted.

That wasn't true, Trace thought. Jade wasn't stubborn. She was an Omega wolf. They did everything in their power to keep peace and harmony in a pack.

Now Jinx was laughing. *That's just what Jade lets everyone believe. She isn't an Omega wolf. She is something altogether different. I taught her to give off the impression she was Omega years ago so the General wouldn't use her gifts against her.*

Trace gritted his teeth together and clenched his hands tightly into fists. He was in pain, a constant pain that never left. His head was pounding, his arms felt like they are going to be pulled from his body, his legs were weak and sharp pains were shooting through them, not to mention what was going on under all the damn chains that were crushing his chest. Growling, he tried to block the pain out so he could respond to Jinx, but it was getting more and more difficult by the minute.

Look, Jinx said, *I know you don't trust me. I would think less of you if you did right now. But I AM Jade's brother. We're on our way to Colombia to find you, but I need to know where you are. Jaxson has looked up everything he can on Perez, and nothing is leading him to you. Angel wasn't able to reach you for some reason. You are stuck with me. Now, you can either tell me where you are, or I will get the information myself.*

Get the information yourself? Trace questioned with a snarl. He did not want someone digging around in his head. If Jinx could do as he suggested against Trace's will, he had to be very powerful.

Yes, get it myself. Make no mistake, I can and I will, Trace. My sister is hurting right now and I won't allow that to continue. Now, for the last time, where are you?

Deciding there was no other option, Trace gave Jinx the information he needed, including the layout of the mansion. Last, he showed Jinx The Dungeon, where he and several other prisoners were being held. *There are two females here that need to come with us,* Trace demanded. *My father has one with him. She's a young girl named Sari who he stole from her family to keep as his mistress. The other is her older sister, Gypsy.* Glancing in the cell next to him, Trace showed Jinx the spot where Gypsy lay. *She is stuck down here with me, beaten daily and starved half to death. I won't leave without them.*

They will come with us, Jinx agreed, letting Trace see the sincerity in his mind. *I will make sure of it. The other prisoners are on their own, though. My top priority is my sister. If shit goes south, I'm getting her the hell out of there.*

Jade? You brought my mate into battle? Trace growled. *What the hell were you thinking?*

I was thinking she would kick my ass if I left her home, Jinx responded sarcastically. *Jade's not one to sit on the sidelines when someone she cares about is in danger. Remember that.*

Trace collapsed as he felt Jinx's sudden withdrawal. Laying his head on his arm, he struggled to stay awake. His body felt like it was on fire and sweat beaded up on his flesh. He had a fever. On top of everything else, he was now infected with some kind of virus. Trace knew then that his body had gone to shit. Shifters didn't get sick. He was in trouble.

Glancing over at Gypsy lying on the hard concrete floor, her legs pulled up and her arms wrapped around them in the fetal position, Trace whispered, "It won't be long now, my friend. I'm getting you out of here." Closing his eyes, he pictured his beautiful mate, praying he would see her soon. He imagined her snuggled close to him, before slowly allowing himself to lose consciousness again.

~

Jade sat in a seat next to Jinx on the plane staring out the window into complete darkness. They had been flying for hours and her wolf was clawing at her, demanding she hurry and find Trace. Lost in thought, she jumped when Jinx grabbed her hand, giving it a quick squeeze before letting go. "I found him," he said with a slow grin. Jade's eyes widened and she grabbed his arm tightly.

"Talk to us, Jinx," Angel ordered as the rest of the team turned in their direction. Jinx's lip curled and a low growl escaped.

"Please, Jinx," Jade begged softly, knowing he was pissed at the authoritative tone in Angel's voice. "We need them."

Glaring at Angel, Jinx snarled, "I take orders from no one."

"You take orders from the General. That piece of shit," Phoenix retorted.

Jinx let out a short, low laugh. "Do I?" he asked with a cocky grin, eyebrows raised. Leaning back in his seat, Jinx nodded to Jaxson. "Trace gave me the coordinates to the place where he is being held. I will send them to you.

Eyes narrowing, Jaxson asked, "Exactly how are you going to…" before he finished his sentence his eyes widened and his fingers started flying over the computer keys. "Thanks man."

Turning to look out the window while Jaxson went to work, Jinx told them, "He's in rough shape. His body is breaking down. He has been held and tortured for so long that if we don't get him out of there soon, he isn't going to make it." At Jade's gasp, he raised his hand and grabbed her chin, forcing her to look in his eyes. "We are going to get him out of there, Jade. I promise you." Sighing, she leaned into him, resting her head on his shoulder. Jade had gone through hell the majority of her life, but nothing had ever scared her as much as the thought of losing Trace. She would take a deep dark hole full of scorpions and rattlers over this fear any day.

"There's more," Jinx continued, glancing up at Angel. "There are two innocent females being held against their will. Trace insists on bringing them back with us. That sick bastard, Perez has made the youngest girl his mistress. The sister, Gypsy, is being held in the cells with Trace."

"Cells?" Angel inquired. "What do you mean by cells?"

"The impression I got was of a basement with approximately 10 steel cells. Big cages really. It was dark, but I could make out prisoners in a number of them, including Gypsy in the one next to Trace. I will be surprised if she makes it. She looked weak and broken. The problem is, Trace won't leave without her. He cares about her. He doesn't really know the sister, but this woman he won't leave behind."

Jade couldn't control her reaction. The thought of her mate going to such lengths to care for and protect another woman had her wolf pissed off. As a growl escaped, her claws punched through her fingertips digging into Jinx's arm. "Stop it, Jade," Jinx ordered roughly. "Stop and think. He has been stuck in that nightmare for months. That woman has been there for him, she's been his rock." At Jade's vicious snarl, he let some of his power out, slowly pushing her wolf back. Jade watched as her claws receded, but even though her wolf had backed off, she was still pissed. "Jade, she is his friend. She has taken beatings that should have been his, stood up for him while he was being tortured. She has a broken arm because she tried to feed him when he was starving. I saw it. I felt the terror in him when he couldn't protect her. But it was never the love of a mate, only the love of a good friend or sister."

Calming at Jinx's explanation, Jade hung her head in shame. She had let jealously get the best of her and become someone she was not proud of. Even though she knew it was because their mating bond wasn't complete, she was still ashamed of her actions.

"I got his location," Jaxson interrupted excitedly. "Holy shit, this place is huge. It's like a fortress. I'm going to see if I can find blueprints for it. Do you know where he is being held?"

"He's in the basement. That's where all of the prisoners are."

"Perez keeps his prisoners in his basement?" Phoenix asked incredulously. "What jackass designed that? Why would you want your enemies right below you?"

"Control," Angel responded grimly. "He wants to know that he has control at all times."

"That's just fucked up," Phoenix spat angrily. "This whole situation is fucked up."

"I agree," Angel responded. "Now, Jinx, if you could please tell us what else you know so we can come up with a plan, I would appreciate it."

Acknowledging her request with a quick nod, Jinx went into detail regarding everything he knew about the place and people in the mansion where Trace was being held. He had a lot of information, because no matter what he might have told Trace, he'd dug deep and came up with all he needed to know to infiltrate the place. Jinx was a soldier. He would use whatever means necessary to extract the information needed and take down an enemy. He didn't care who he crossed or pissed off in the process, as long as he got the job done.

By the time the plane landed an hour later, a plan was in effect and RARE was ready to roll. Jade insisted she be a part of not only planning the mission, but also the rescue itself. They were not leaving her out. With Jinx backing her, RARE had no choice except to agree, knowing the twins would go off on their own if they didn't. The only requirement Angel made was that Jade stick close to either Angel or Jinx. Jade let Angel think she was in agreement, but if she had to get to Trace, she would do so no matter what. She was not going to sit around and wait for someone to hold her hand.

Chapter 7

Trace jerked awake to the painful sound of Gypsy retching. She had somehow managed to drag herself to the far side of her cell and proceeded to empty her stomach of the small portion of food she'd forced herself to consume that morning. The same thing happened when she'd eaten three days before. Her body was rejecting nourishment now and she was slowly starving to death.

As she sobbed quietly in the corner, her entire body shaking with chills, Trace whispered into her mind, *It's ok, girl. My friends are on their way. We're getting out of here soon.*

Trace had discovered there was a reason the woman was named Gypsy. She had certain gifts herself that she'd never been allowed to share with anyone, not even Sari. Gypsy's mother met her father at the young age of 17 and they fell instantly in love. They were married just two years later and that's when he shared his secret. He had gypsy blood in his veins. He thought of it as magic. Magic that was passed to his daughter when she was born. After her father was murdered by modern day witch hunters when Gypsy was four, her mother grabbed her and fled. Eight years later, her mother met and came to care deeply for Sari's father. They were married within six months and Gypsy was legally adopted by her stepfather. For the first time in several years, both Gypsy and her mother felt safe. Then, several years later, Philip Perez killed Gypsy's family, all except Sari whom he held as a mistress now, and ruined her life.

Although Gypsy hadn't shared with Trace exactly what her gifts were, she'd slipped up and used telepathy with him on his first torture session. That was now Trace and Gypsy's preferred means of communication as long as they were strong enough to hold the link. There were cameras in The Dungeon and Trace did not want his father's men catching them talking.

Did you hear me, Gypsy? Trace asked. *We're getting out of here. My friends are near.*

It hurts, Gypsy responded weakly. *Everything hurts. I just want the pain to go away. Why are they doing this? Why?*

Trace had shared parts of his past with Gypsy. There was nothing to do but talk on the days they were left alone over the past few months. They talked to try and focus on something besides the pain and heartache they were enduring. They talked to remind themselves they were still alive and could. He hadn't told her everything about his past. She didn't know the details regarding his escape with his mother and Starr. She also didn't know how deeply involved he'd been with his father's cartel before his escape. Some information he trusted no one with. Not even RARE. However, he did tell her what it was like growing up as the son of a notorious drug lord. He'd told her about barely making it through some days. How when he was just eight years old, Trace's father ordered his men to beat the hell out of Trace; to do whatever it took to make him a man. Trace suffered weekly beatings until finally he was strong enough to fight back. Gypsy knew Trace was a shifter. He couldn't hide it from her after she was moved into the cell next to his. Trace had to fight his cat not to take over during the torture sessions, and when he was put back in his cell he couldn't fully keep his cat in. Sometimes his eyes went panther or his claws would come out, but Trace would fight it. The chains surrounding him were bound too tight to allow Trace to shift. He would only injure himself and possibly not be able to shift back. Trace also told Gypsy about Jade. She knew Trace was fighting to get back to his mate and she vowed to help him get to her. Gypsy constantly encouraged Trace to fight, to survive. Now she needed someone to encourage her.

They'll be here soon, Gypsy. Trace promised her. *Then we will take you home. There's a doctor there, Doc Josie. She's with the White River wolf pack. She will take care of you. You push through that pain, Gypsy. You show me how you fight. You show me that gypsy magic.*

I'm too weak, she whispered back. *I can't use my magic.*

Yes you can, Trace promised. *You can use it if you need to defend yourself, and you will. You are stronger than you think, Gypsy.* Closing his eyes tightly, Trace took a deep breath. Fighting to push away the roaring pain in his head, he continued. *Let me tell you about my team.*

Team? Gypsy asked confused. With everything they'd discussed, Trace hadn't mentioned RARE. But he figured now would be the time to do it since his team was about to make an appearance. She needed to know she could trust his teammates to get them out of there. She'd been through so much already, he didn't want her to be terrified of them too.

Yes, my team. We call ourselves RARE. It stands for Rescue And Retrieval Extractions. That's what we do, Gypsy. We find people that have been kidnapped and we rescue them. My team will find us. They'll get us out of here, he promised.

You never told me about them, she said softly. *You were protecting them.*

They're my family, he responded. *I will protect them with my life.* Slowly, Gypsy raised her head and looked at him. Reaching out, she carefully, painfully, inched her way back over to his cell.

Tell me about them, she said weakly as she pushed herself into a sitting position and leaned back against the hard concrete wall. *Tell me what they are like.*

Well, Angel is our leader, our Alpha, he started. *She's tough as nails and you obey her orders or you are out. But she's fair and she is the first one there if anyone messes with her family. That's what we are, a family.* Smiling ruefully, he said, *Angel is also the first one to kick your ass if you mess up. Nico is her right hand man. He found his mate back in April when her daughter, Lily, was kidnapped by the General...*

The General? Gypsy interrupted in confusion. *Aren't generals good guys in the army or something?*

Growling lowly, Trace said, *Normally they are, but this guy is as messed up as they come. A psychotic son of a bitch that gets off on having his men beat and rape women. He has some kind of breeding program going on...* At Gypsy's startled gasp, Trace decided he'd better start at the beginning. As he told Gypsy about their first encounter with the General he silently prayed his team would get there soon. He didn't know how much longer he could hold out.

Chapter 8

RARE fanned out, making their way silently through the jungle under the cover of the night. Jade made sure she was on Jinx's six like he'd taught her years ago. No matter what anyone else thought, this wasn't her first mission. She'd gone with Jinx on several ops, none sanctioned by the General, of course. The General had no idea what Jade was capable of. If he did, he would be fighting a lot harder to get her back.

They were a mile out from the mansion and the closer they got, the harder it was getting for Jade to control her wolf who wanted to get to Trace now. *I need help,* she admitted reluctantly to Jinx. As much as she wanted to prove to the team that she could handle the mission, right now if she didn't get her wolf under control she would blow the op for everyone.

Stopping abruptly, Jinx faced her and put both hands on her shoulders. Looking directly into her eyes, he growled deeply, once again letting out some of his power and forcing Jade's wolf back. After several precious minutes, Jade rested her hands on Jinx's and squeezed lightly. Without a word, they continued on as one to their destination.

When they were 500 yards out the team slowed their pace, moving stealthily and keeping an eye out for the enemy. Taking her sniper rifle, Rikki scaled a tree, finding a place to hide in its branches just a couple hundred yards from the main gate surrounding the estate. Storm took up residence in another tree just south of Rikki. Normally Storm preferred to be in the middle of the action, but even though Doc Josie cleared her for duty, she stressed that Storm needed to stay as much on the sidelines for this mission as possible. That was okay, Storm rocked at sniper duty as well. Both women were locked and loaded and ready to start picking off guards when Angel gave the order.

The team had decided their best course of action was to take out the guards on the back side of the mansion, then scale the fence to gain access. *Now,* Angel ordered. Rikki and Storm made quick work of the guards, before scurrying back down the trees and moving to new positions at the front of the mansion and on the West side. Ryker was already in position on the East side. The object was to surround the building with snipers and take out as many guards as they could while the rest of RARE infiltrated through the back.

Take them out, Angel ordered. As guards started falling, Angel growled, *Go!* Not waiting for the rest of RARE, Jade swiftly followed Jinx up and over the fence and stayed on his six until they reached the backdoor of the mansion. Glancing back, she saw the rest of the team had also scaled the fence. Phoenix and Jaxson quickly moved to separate sides of the building and started setting the bombs, rigging it to blow.

Knowing she wouldn't be able to keep Jade from finding her mate once they breached the walls of the mansion, Angel had given Jinx, Jade and Flame instructions to go directly to the basement for Trace and Gypsy. Angel and Nico were going to find Sari. Silently, they entered the mansion, Jinx quickly snapped the neck of the guard standing right inside the door. Motioning for Jade and Flame to follow, Jinx headed down a long hallway with plush, dark red carpet. The sound of a television greeted them as they reached a living room. Jinx stopped, holding up his hand. Jade and Flame waited as Jinx slipped his sword from the scabbard on his back. Silently he crept up on the two men standing by a window. One was looking out it while the other was frantically talking into a cell phone, gesturing wildly with one arm. They were obviously aware the estate had been infiltrated.

Jade watched unemotionally as the blade of Jinx's sword severed first one head and then the other. These men hurt her mate. They deserved exactly what they got. Wiping the blood off his sword on one of the men's shirts, Jinx turned and continued into the kitchen area right off the living room, a stunned Flame following. Stopping at the door leading down to The Dungeon, Jinx looked back at the women. "There are three men down there right now, unaware of what is happening up here. They are getting ready to work Trace over again."

Jade palmed her Glock and growled, "I'm ready."

"We got this," Flame snarled, pulling out a knife from a sheath on her leg. Jinx tried the door, finding it locked from the inside. With one last look at Jade and Flame, he slammed his shoulder into the door smashing it inward off the hinges. Scaling the stairs in two leaps, he took the head of one of the men fighting to get Trace on the table with a quick slice of his sword. Shocked, one of the other men dropped a clamp he had in his hand and ran past Jinx to the stairs. Flame took him out on her way down, with a knife to the heart. The last man standing snarled, "Bring it on you sons of bitches," as he pulled out a gun to shoot. Jade put three bullets in his heart before he could pull the trigger. The gun slipped from his fingers as he fell lifelessly to the floor.

Jinx sheathed his sword and grabbed Trace before he could drop to the ground. Trace struggled as Jinx tried to lift him onto the table to get his chains off.

Running to him, Jade framed Trace's face with her hands, tears streaming down her cheeks. "It's okay, Trace. It's okay, my mate."

Trace slowly stopped struggling at the sound of her voice. Forcing his swollen eyes to open, he drank in the sight of Jade standing in front of him. "You're here," he whispered huskily. "You're really here." Slowly he collapsed to the ground, dragging Jade down with him.

Releasing a tortured sob, Jade ran her hands over Trace's head, then lightly down his sunken cheeks while placing small, gentle kisses on his dried, cracked lips. "I'm here," she told him as she nuzzled his neck, stiffening when her body came into contact with the thick chains surrounding him. Leaning back, she turned to Jinx and growled, "Get them off."

"Guard the stairs, Flame," Jinx ordered, the commanding tone of his voice leaving no room for argument. "No one gets down them, understood?" Flame gave a quick nod and moved to the bottom of the stairs, her weapon drawn and ready.

Kneeling down next to them, Jinx quickly started to unwrap the heavy chain from Trace's left arm. "This is going to hurt like a bitch, man," he murmured. "Your cat is going to try and take over, but you have to fight through the pain and stop him.

He just wants to protect you, but he could hurt someone on accident."

Trace groaned as Jinx got his left arm unwrapped and moved to work on his right arm. Sweat beaded up on Trace's forehead and a growl escaped when Jinx started removing the chain from his chest. "Breathe through the pain, Trace," Jinx snarled when Trace's fangs punched through his gums and he let out a roar of agony. "Block it out."

"What's going on," Jade demanded, the fear evident in her voice.

"The chains have been constricting him for months, Jade. Now that I am removing them, the pain feels like it is crushing him. But I have to get them off. We can't get him out of here like this." After finally unraveling the last of the chains, Jinx paused and placed a hand firmly on Trace's shoulder. "Look at me, Trace," he commanded.

Trace raised his head, his dark eyes flashing, and roared again. He struggled to hold his body tightly in check, fighting his cat. Jade gently stroked a hand down his arm trying to help calm him. "Look at me," Jinx demanded again forcefully. When Trace's eyes met his, Jinx grabbed hold of his shoulders and growled, "You will stand down. You will get yourself under control. I will not allow you to hurt Jade." Trace seemed to freeze at the mention of his mate.

As Jade watched, Trace fought valiantly for control. With Jinx's help, he finally won several long agonizing minutes later. Sagging under the pain and exhaustion, Trace laid down on the hard floor, his head in Jade's lap. She gently continued to run her hands over his body, trying to soothe him with her touch. Jade bent down to kiss Trace softly on his cheek, once again nuzzling his neck. She cried softly as Trace shuddered, pain racing through his body.

"Trace," Jade heard a tentative female voice call out weakly. "Trace, where are you?" Jade lifted her head as she heard movement in one of the cells. "Don't hurt him, you bastards. Don't you hurt him anymore," the voice cried out.

"Gypsy," Jade whispered as Trace fought to sit up and respond. Jinx leaned over and helped Jade pull Trace into a sitting position before standing and moving toward the woman. She continued to yell and threaten them as she tried to pull herself up using the bars on her cage. Jade's heart went out to the woman that fought to help Trace. Her tremendous courage, in spite of the situation, was amazing. Just hours before Jade had been extremely jealous of Gypsy, but seeing her now, all she felt was empathy for her.

Jinx stopped in front of Gypsy and lightly touched her hand that was closed tightly around the steel bar. "Calm down, little one. You are safe now. No one will harm you again. You are going home."

Tears fell down Gypsy's filthy cheeks as she watched Jinx, her face full of hope. Her voice quivered as she asked, "Are you one of Trace's teammates?" Gently, Jinx shook his head.

"No, Jinx isn't. But I am," Jade rushed to assure the woman as Gypsy started to scoot back in fear. "My name is Jade, Gypsy. And I want to thank you for helping my mate through this horrible ordeal."

"This is all happy and wonderful," Flame interjected from her position by the stairs, "But I vote you grab the keys from the dead guy, unlock the prisoners, and we get the hell out of here."

"Agreed," Jinx said. Moving swiftly, he unhooked the keys from the belt on one of the guards and after finding the right key, he unlocked Gypsy's door. Moving to the next cell, he unlocked it and threw the keys at the prisoner. "Unlock the rest of the cells down here before you leave this room," he ordered. "You will not leave until that is done."

As the severely injured man managed to crawl out of the cell and move to the next one, Jinx went back to Gypsy and gently lifted her into his arms.

"Can you walk?" he asked as he glanced over to see Trace had made it to his feet with Jade's help. Meeting Jinx's eyes, Trace growled, "Let's go."

"What about Sari?" Gypsy whispered as she laid her head tiredly against Jinx's shoulder. "We have to get Sari."

"Already being taken care of," Jinx responded as they headed up the stairs, Flame taking the lead.

Chapter 9

Angel and Nico swiftly cleared room after room on the second floor. There was no sign of Sari on the first floor, and so far none on the second floor either. "Shit," Nico yelled as they heard the sound of a helicopter on the roof. As Angel opened the door to what looked like the master bedroom, they quickly cleared the room together before running to the doors by the balcony. *Do you have eyes on the target?* Angel demanded as she peeked through the curtains covering the large windows. *Do not let him get on the chopper. I repeat, do not let him get on that damn chopper. You take him out!*

On it boss, was Rikki's quiet response right before she took one shot, quickly followed by another. *Two down. I don't have a shot on the third.*

Got him, Storm said as she took out the third man. *All men on the roof are down.*

Hearing a soft whimper, Angel swung around in the direction of the noise and quickly closed the distance to the closed bathroom door. Knocking softly she called out, "Sari. Sari, honey, my name is Angel. Trace and Gypsy sent me to get you out of here." Angel frowned as she heard the soft whimper again, but no other response.

Slowly Angel opened the door, afraid of what she would find on the other side. Hiding in the bathtub, a large kitchen knife in one hand, was a young, terrified girl. She was naked and shaking so hard Angel was worried she might accidentally cut herself. *Stay back, Nico,* she whispered as she cautiously moved toward the child. *There is no danger in here. Just a scared child. Find me some clothes for her, quickly.*

Kneeling down on the floor in front of the tub, Angel smiled gently at the girl. "You are Sari, right?" she asked even though she knew this was Gypsy's sister. "You're going to be okay, Sweetheart. I promise. I'm here to take you home."

Sari shook her head sadly, her beautiful dark brown eyes filling with tears. "I don't have a home anymore," she whispered in a tortured voice. "That asshole took it from me. He took everything from me."

"Not everything," Angel responded as she reached out and gently removed the sharp knife from Sari's fingers. "You still have Gypsy."

Eyes widening, Sari rasped, "Gypsy's still alive?" Grasping the side of the tub, she moved to her knees and then painfully pulled herself up until she was standing, leaning back against the wall. There were bruises covering the majority of Sari's body and Angel was worried she might have internal damage the way she was moving.

Helping Sari step out of the bathtub on her trembling legs, Angel promised her, "Gypsy is very much alive, Sari. My team is getting her as we speak."

"Philip told me she was dead," Sari whispered raggedly. "He told me he killed her because I wouldn't cooperate. But I did everything he said. I tried to be good. I really did."

I have clothes, boss, Nico said, his voice full of barely controlled rage. *I'm going to leave them on the floor outside the door and go wait in the hallway so I don't scare her any more than she already is.*

As soon as she knew Nico was gone, Angel turned and opened the door to the bathroom. Reaching down, she grabbed Sari's clothes and quickly shut the door again. "Here are some clothes, Sari. Hurry and get dressed so we can get out of here."

"Don't leave me," Sari burst out as Angel went to open the door again. Rushing forward, Sari grabbed her stomach crying out in pain. "Please, she begged on a sob, "please, don't leave me."

"I won't go anywhere," Angel promised as she shut the door and leaned up against it, crossing her arms over her chest. Waiting for Sari to get ready, Angel frowned and gently entered her mind to try and figure out why she was in so much pain.

Angel tightly grasped her arms and smothered a growl when she was swamped with pain, sadness and despair. From the faint impressions she got, it seemed as if Sari had somehow pissed Perez off recently and he'd repeatedly beaten her, throwing her on the floor and kicking her in the stomach over and over. When he was done, he left her to fend for herself. She was alone, in excruciating pain, and scared to death. Angel was going to kill the bastard slowly, if he wasn't already dead.

As soon as Sari was ready, Angel opened the door and motioned for her to follow. Softly she whispered, "My teammate, Nico, is waiting outside. He will not hurt you, Sari. You can trust him. We will get you out of here."

When Sari stopped suddenly and moaned again clutching her stomach, Angel turned and caught her just before she fell to the ground. *Nico, get in here,* she ordered. *I need your help.*

Angel put Sari in Nico's arms when he stepped in the room and they swiftly left heading down the hall. *Are you clear?* She asked Jade as they took the stairs leading down to the back entryway.

I need help with Trace, Jade responded. *He's having trouble walking and Jinx is carrying Gypsy.*

Phoenix, if you are done playing with your toys, get your ass in here and get our boy, Angel ordered as they reached the back door.

Swinging around, gun raised, she waited patiently after hearing footsteps in the next room. *It's just us,* Flame said as she led the way to where Angel waited. Jinx was right behind her carrying a small, frail, filthy woman who had lost consciousness. Angel gulped as she saw Jade helping Trace make his way painfully down the hall. He was so thin and gaunt and was obviously in a lot of pain. His feet shuffled slowly along the carpet, his arm around Jade's shoulder. His head hung low as if he didn't have the strength to hold it up and his shoulders slumped. She was really going to kill that fucking bastard, Perez. No one messed with her family. No one. Turning, Angel ran back up the stairs to the second floor entering the first bedroom. Pulling a blanket off the bed, she quickly returned to Trace and wrapped his naked, shivering form in the warm material.

I'm here, boss, Phoenix said as the back door opened and he slipped through. One look at Trace and Phoenix was in the room lifting him into his arms. "I can walk dammit," Trace insisted sluggishly, pushing weakly against Phoenix.

"Yeah, well I can run and this place is set to blow soon," Phoenix replied with a grimace. "How about we get these women the hell out of here?" Not able to argue against that logic, Trace gave in sullenly.

Guards are all down, Angel, Rikki said. *Jaxson has the gates open and is waiting out front in a truck.*

They exited quickly out the back and made their way to the front, sticking to the side of the mansion just in case there were any guards they'd missed. Seeing the truck with Jaxson at the wheel, Angel raced forward and jumped in the truck bed, the others following. After helping them in, Angel sat down and pulled a terrified Sari into her arms. Jaxson sped through the gates, stopping to let Ryker get in front with him while Storm and Rikki hopped in back. They held on tight as Jaxson raced through the jungle on the rough dirt road to get to their plane.

"Did you get him?" Angel asked Rikki as Sari snuggled into her side, her eyes never leaving Gypsy. "Was he on that helicopter?"

"No," Rikki shook her head. "It wasn't Perez."

"He isn't here," Sari told them, as a tear slipped down her cheek. She clutched her stomach and cried out as they hit another pothole. Angel tugged her closer and ran a comforting hand down Sari's long, dark hair.

"He wasn't here?" Angel asked. Damn, she'd hoped the prick was already dead. "Where the hell is he?"

"He left yesterday," Sari whispered. "He never tells me where he is going. All I heard him say was he had a lead on someone named Sophia. I don't know who that is, though."

Well, shit, Angel thought. He was going after Trace's mother. They were going to have to get to her first. Trace had been through too much. Angel refused to let him lose his mother and sister, too. First they were going to have to get home and regroup. They would get their wounded to Doc Josie to be taken care of. Then RARE would do what they did best. They'd get to Trace's family, retrieve them, and bring them home. Angel was done messing with Philip Perez. Once Sophia and Starr were safe, RARE was going hunting.

Chapter 10

Thankfully, Nico had some strong pain medicine on the plane that helped ease Trace's discomfort enough so he could finally fall into a deep, healing sleep. As much as Jade wanted to talk with him and assure herself he was okay, she was content with holding him against her on the floor in the back of the plane and vowing to never let him go. Rubbing her cheek on the top of his head where it rested on her chest, she closed her eyes and savored the feel of him in her arms. It was going to take a long time to recover from everything his body had been put through, but the important thing was that he was safe and with her now.

I'm leaving as soon as the plane lands, Jinx said softly into her mind. Jade stiffened and raised her head to look at her brother sitting in a seat in the back of the plane. He stared straight ahead, and even though he didn't move his head, she knew he was aware of everything that happened on the plane. *I have to get back before the General gets suspicious.*

I don't want you to go, Jade whispered as she lowered her head letting her hair fall forward to hide the tears welling up in her eyes.

I don't have a choice, sis, you know that. Someone needs to be on the inside to take the General down. That someone is me. Jade felt Jinx's determination and knew there would be no talking him out of going back. She was proud of her brother. He could have turned out so differently given the hand life had dealt him. Instead he was a strong, loyal and loving brother. He knew right from wrong and chose to do what was right, even knowing it could get him killed. *Right back at ya,* Jinx muttered.

Stop doing that! She growled. *You are only allowed to talk to me this way. You are not allowed to get inside my head.*

Jinx chuckled out loud causing the people nearest him to glance his way. Ignoring them, he responded, *I had to make sure you were ok. I'm satisfied now.*

The rest of the trip was spent in silence. Trace woke up right as the plane touched down. He was in excruciating pain, but Nico was able to give him more pain medicine to help dull it. As soon as they exited the plane, Jinx was gone. *Make sure and get rid of that motorcycle,* he said right before he vanished.

Seriously, who rides a motorcycle in the dead of winter, Jade grumbled. She hid a secret smile as Jinx's laughter washed over her.

~

Gypsy didn't wake up during the plane ride, nor did she gain consciousness on the ride to the White River Wolves compound. Nico called ahead to fill Chase, the Alpha for the White River Wolves, in on the situation so they were not stopped at the gates, while Ryker contacted his mate to make sure she was ready for them. Arriving at the hospital, they were met out front by Doc Josie and several nurses. "Get them all inside," the doctor ordered briskly as she headed to the SUV where Trace was sitting with the door open. "Get the woman cleaned up while I look at Trace."

"No," Trace refused immediately. "You take care of Gypsy first."

"Actually, I think you need to look at Sari first, Doc," Angel interrupted as she gently guided the young, frightened woman forward. Her face was pure white and she was holding tightly to her stomach. Suddenly, Sari cried out and doubled over in pain as dark red blood soaked through her tan pants. Eyes widening, Jade stood in shock as Chase suddenly appeared behind Sari and gently scooped her up in his arms. Ignoring Angel who stood frozen beside Sari, Chase quickly made his way up the hospital steps and through the doors, Doc Josie following close behind. Trace watched curiously as Angel gazed longingly after Chase before masking her emotions with a scowl. Chase was Angel's mate, but she'd been fighting the mate bond when Trace left. Obviously she still was.

When Phoenix tried to lift Trace out of the vehicle, Trace decided he'd had enough. He was going to walk into the damn hospital if it killed him. He was a fighter, not a victim. Snarling at Phoenix, Trace stepped out of the vehicle on his own, standing beside it for several minutes to catch his breath. Jade appeared beside him, slipping an arm around his waist and giving him a sweet smile. This he could handle. Sliding an arm over her shoulder, Trace let Jade guide him slowly up the stairs and into the hospital. They followed a nurse into one of the rooms, but when Jade started toward the bed, Trace balked. "I want a shower," he insisted. "I need one badly."

When the nurse would have protested, Jade simply turned directions and walked with Trace into the bathroom. Trace allowed her to help him sit down on the toilet to rest while she turned on the shower. "Get it as hot as you can," Trace muttered tiredly from where he sat. "I have several months of filth and grime covering me. The closest I came to a shower was when they turned the hose on me during torture sessions."

Trace watched as Jade checked the steaming water to make sure it wouldn't burn him, before turning to glance in his direction. With hooded eyes, he secretly took in her hot, sexy body.

Moving back to the door, Jade shut it on the shocked nurse. Turning, she seemed to be contemplating something. Coming to a decision, she grabbed the hem of her shirt and slipped it over her head. Undoing the button on her pants, she slid the zipper down and shimmied out of them. Looking nervously at Trace, she froze when their eyes connected. Blushing, she slipped her fingers into the waist band of her panties and slowly slid them down. Trace groaned as he watched Jade bite down on her bottom lip. His breath quickened and he hardened instantly at the thought of those pretty, pink lips wrapped around his dick. Slowly, Jade reached back and unhooked her bra, removing it and placing it with the rest of her clothes.

Trace took in the beautiful sight of his mate, and couldn't believe fate had gifted him with the vision before him. Long blonde hair, dark green eyes, small, pert breasts that would just fill the palm of his hand. Trace was aware his gaze now held the look of a predator, but he couldn't control it. Jade took a tentative step back, exciting him further. The panther in him wanted her to run. He loved a good chase. But Trace didn't want to scare her.

"Don't run," Trace growled, his eyes narrowing. "It will just excite my cat." Standing, he shrugged off the blanket that still covered his body. "You are so damn beautiful, Jade. So perfect," he groaned as he reached out and gently cupped one small, creamy white breast in the palm of his hand. Gasping, Jade shivered and cried out as he ran his thumb over her nipple, before lowering his head and tugging it into his mouth. Jade whimpered as Trace swirled his tongue around the nipple, then tugged on it gently with his teeth. Pulling back, he softly nipped his way up her neck and whispered into her ear, "I want to fuck you, Jade. I want to bury myself so deep inside you that you can't stop screaming my name. But not here, not like this."

Jade trembled uncontrollably when Trace stepped back, tugging on her hand for her to follow. Pulling the curtain aside, he stepped into the large, square shower under the hot spray, moaning in pure pleasure. His whole body ached in pain from the brutal punishment it had taken over the past several months, except for his dick. That ached for a different reason. But the hot water soothed the aches and pains, and made him feel alive again. It had been so long since he'd felt hot water. Bracing himself against the sides of the shower, he bowed his head and let the water roll over him.

Suddenly, Trace froze as Jade stepped in the shower and shut the curtain behind her. He moaned as he felt her soft hands on his skin, and kept as still as possible as she lathered his back with soap.

Taking her time, his mate washed every inch of his backside before moving around to the front. Running her hands over his chest, she traced his tattoo of two sniper rifles on the right side of his chest before lightly tweaking his nipples. After getting more soap, she knelt down to wash his legs. When he didn't think he could stand it any longer, she took his rock hard length into her small hands, stroking him slowly before moving one hand down to gently message his balls. A bolt of pleasure shot through him, and a growl of need escaped.

Breathing heavily, his arms trembling, Trace rasped, "Jade, you need to stop." She leaned back, smiling tentatively up at him, as she allowed the shower to wash the suds from his body. Then, before he could move, she was back taking his hard cock in her hand and wrapping her soft pink lips around the tip. Trace's hips jerked, and he groaned loudly as his cock was encased in the hot, velvet heat of her mouth. Looking down into her large, innocent eyes, he started to pull out, but Jade grasped his ass with her hands and refused to let him. "You don't have to do this, baby," he whispered.

Pulling back, she rasped. "I want to, Trace. Teach me."

Oh God, he thought as he fought not to come right then. How could he deny his beautiful mate anything at the moment? Letting go of the wall on one side, he reached down and slipped his fingers into her mass of wavy locks. "Slowly," he murmured as he guided her lips back to him. He knew he wasn't going to last long, but he was going to savor the pleasure for as long as possible. Her gaze filled with hunger, Jade traced her lips with her tongue and moved closer until Trace tightened his hand in her hair forcing her to stop. Glancing up in surprise, eyes wide and lips slightly parted, Jade gasped when Trace guided his dick past her soft, wet lips. Jade moaned as Trace slowly began to push in and out of her sweet, warm mouth.

Jade's moans of pleasure finally put him over the edge. Feeling his orgasm building, Trace let go of the wall, tangling his other hand in her hair and holding her still while he drove into her mouth over and over again. When Jade dug her nails into his ass with one hand while tugging on his balls with the other, Trace came on a roar, filling her mouth. He watched in satisfaction as she took it all.

Sliding down on the tile beside Jade moments later, Trace pulled her close, placing a kiss on the top of her head. Letting his eyes drift close, he whispered, "Thank you, love."

Chapter 11

Chase stood by his office window watching the sun go down. His mate was here, on his land, where she belonged. Raking a hand through his short black hair, he swore savagely. Yeah, she was here. Until she knew Trace was okay. Then she would leave. She always left. While their unclaimed mating was eating him alive, she was doing everything in her power to avoid him.

He stiffened when Angel's scent suddenly surrounded him. Groaning, he placed one hand against the window and leaned his head against the cool glass. "Chase," she said from the doorway.

Feeling his fangs drop, Chase squeezed his eyes tightly shut and fought his wolf who wanted to claim her now. "What," he asked, not bothering to turn around. There was only so much he could take, and he was almost to his breaking point.

"I would like to see the girls," Angel said as she moved further into the room. "I haven't seen them in days." Back in May, RARE rescued two women and three children from a facility in Mexico where they were being held by the General. One of the children, a bear shifter named Hunter, was adopted by Phoenix and Serenity. Angel had fallen in love with the other two children, beautiful twin girls, Hope and Faith. She was unable to take care of them with her lifestyle, so Chase welcomed the girls into his home, hoping his mate would soon follow. Angel came to see them as often as possible, but her responsibilities with RARE kept her busy.

"You know you can see them whenever you want, Angel," Chase said as he slowly raised his head to look out the window again. The beauty in the thousands of acres of land behind his office helped calm him. "They're at the daycare right now. I was just going to go pick them up and take them home for dinner and baths."

"I can do it," Angel offered. Her voice was getting closer, her scent overpowering. His dick hardened painfully and he cursed under his breath.

"Fine," Chase responded shortly. "I have a few things I need to do before I get home. I will be there in a couple of hours so you can get back to the hospital."

"Look Chase," Angel said from right beside him. Before he could stop himself, Chase grabbed her waist and turned her quickly, pushing her up against the window. Breathing raggedly, he stared into her mesmerizing, lust filled gaze. He wasn't the only one affected by the bond.

Raising her arms above her head and holding them against the window, Chase groaned as he rested the bottom half of his body into hers, his throbbing erection straining against her. He took her mouth roughly with his, slipping his tongue past her lips when she gasped in surprise. When Angel tugged against his hands, trying to free herself, Chase growled in warning. Pulling back, he licked his way down her neck, gently scraping it with his fangs.

"I can't, Chase," Angel breathed even as she arched into him. "I can't do this."

"Don't act like you don't want me, Angel," Chase snarled, pushing his cock against her roughly. "I can feel your heat through your jeans. I can smell your lust. You want me. You want this."

Angel cried out when Chase nipped her ear, a shiver racing over her body. "Please, Chase. I can't. Not now."

Chase froze, leaning back he asked, "Not now? Then when? I've waited long enough, Angel. I want to hold my mate, dammit!"

"I have never lied to you, Chase," Angel growled, trying to pull away from him. "I never wanted a mate. I told you that. I have so many things in my life that need to come first. I have to go track down Trace's family so they aren't executed by his piece of shit dad. Then I need to hunt down the

General so that my children are safe. So that my son is free. I don't have time to deal with a mate right now, too!"

Tearing himself away from her, Chase walked to the door. Turning around, he asked, "Did it ever occur to you that you don't have to do those things alone? I am your fucking mate, Angel. If you would give me a chance, I would fight by your side."

Before she could respond, he was gone. Chase refused to beg. He was an Alpha, dammit. Alphas did not beg. Removing his clothes and shifting as soon as he was out of the building, Chase headed to the outer boundaries of his land. There had been a breach the month earlier and one of the children was abducted. Doc Josie was out running and managed to save the cub before he was taken off pack lands, but Chase feared it was only the beginning. Someone had found out about his wolf pack, which meant there was a strong possibility others knew, too. Chase added more guards to patrol the area and staggered their schedules so they weren't always in the same place at the same time. He also put himself on the list to patrol whenever possible. Even though he wasn't scheduled, tonight was going to be one of those nights. If he didn't get as far away from Angel as possible, he was going to do something they might both regret.

Chapter 12

Jade gently nudged Trace awake after hearing a noise in the outer room. When he looked at her groggily, she smiled. "We need to get you out of here and into bed," she said softly as she gently ran her fingertips down his cheek. "Unless you would like Phoenix to come back and carry you?"

Shaking his head, Trace struggled to his feet with Jade's help. "That bastard isn't seeing me naked," he muttered.

Chuckling, Jade said, "Good. Let's get dried off and get you into bed. You need rest." After shutting off the water, Jade pulled back the curtain and grabbed a towel. Gently she dried Trace's body, mindful of the bruising and any open wounds. Tears streamed down her face as she thought about the hell he must have endured. When he was dry, Jade quickly stepped out and dried herself off before pulling on her clothes. Going back to where Trace waited, Jade cupped his face and kissed his lips. Frowning, she pulled back and felt his forehead with the back of her hand. "Do you have a fever?" she asked. "I thought you were warm before, but you are extremely hot now. Is it from the shower?"

Trace sighed and lightly urged Jade to the door. Following her slowly, he grabbed onto of the sink to help hold himself up. "It's a fever," he said as he shuffled from the sink to the door. Quickly wrapping a towel around his waist, Jade slid an arm around him and helped him through the door and to the bed.

Rikki stood by the window lost in thought, a wistful look on her face. Her long, black hair was in a thick braid down her back. She was dressed in a black fleece sweater, camo pants and black combat boots. She wore a 9mm at her hip, and Jade knew she had several knives hidden on her as well. The feeling of sorrow and despair radiating from Rikki was disturbing. Jade caught the glimpse of the same handsome, dark haired man that she'd seen before in Rikki's mind before shutting the image out. It wasn't fair to Rikki to delve in her personal life without her knowledge. However, she could help with the emotions that were bombarding Rikki.

Trace immediately fell asleep once he was settled in bed under the warm covers. Jade kissed him tenderly on the forehead before walking over to Rikki and lightly touching her arm. Slowly she started pushing calming energy Rikki's way. After a few moments Rikki whispered, "What did you do to me?"

"I helped you," was all Jade would tell her. They stood there in silence for several minutes before Rikki whispered, "I don't understand why he doesn't want me."

"He?" Jade questioned as she slid an arm around Rikki's shoulders, hugging her as she pushed more soothing vibes in her direction. Rikki and Flame were the closest thing to friends Jade had ever had. She hated to see Rikki suffering.

Sighing deeply, Rikki pulled out of Jade's embrace and sat down in the chair next to them. "His name's Jeremiah. Jeremiah Black."

"The man with the FBI?" Jade asked in surprise.

"Yeah, him," Rikki responded as she stared at the floor refusing to meet Jade's eyes. "When I was captured by the General, he came on the rescue mission with RARE. I was shocked to see him, to be honest, because all he'd ever done before was give us our orders." Looking up at Jade, Rikki whispered, "I heard Jaxson say Jeremiah is my mate."

"Oh, Rikki," Jade murmured as she knelt in front of her. No wonder Rikki was so upset. Even though she was human, she would still feel the pull toward her mate. And she would feel the rejection when he didn't claim her. "Wait," Jade said in confusion. "How long have you known Jeremiah?"

"I don't know? Three years, almost four," Rikki said. "I didn't actually meet him at first. Angel always dealt with him over the phone. But after one rescue, he met us at the airport when we arrived back at the hangar. He wanted to personally pick up the man for some reason." Clearing her throat, Rikki continued softly, "I felt something almost immediately for him, but I didn't know what it was. It got worse every time he came around, which was more often after that first meeting. He was so damn sexy, and…well, I tried to mask my desire as much as I could. I knew he was a shifter and I didn't want him to know how I felt." Raising a pain filled gaze to Jade, Rikki whispered, "He never once acted like he cared. Never looked at me, never touched me. But he cared enough to be a part of the mission to save me. Then he just left. I haven't heard from him since. If he cared enough to come to Arizona, why did he leave me, Jade? Why hasn't he been to see me?"

Leaning forward, Jade gently ran a hand down Rikki's long braid, trying to give her the comfort she so obviously needed. "I don't know, Rikki," she said softly, "but I can tell you why I think he is staying away if it will help."

"Please," Rikki whispered. "God, I feel like such a girl," she spat, wiping at the tears running down her cheeks.

"It's the mating bond," Doc Josie said quietly from the doorway. As Rikki made a move to get up, Josie held up a hand. "Please, sit down, Rikki. I'm so sorry I interrupted. But it's very important that you know what your mate is going through right now and why he has stayed away." Josie moved to kneel down in front of Rikki next to Jade. "I will let Jade explain and will be here to fill in the blanks."

Swallowing hard, Rikki nodded. "Ok," she whispered. "At least maybe this ache will go away if I know why he doesn't want me," she said as she pressed her palm into her chest.

"Oh, Rikki," Jade murmured, "It isn't that he doesn't want you. He wants you too much." At Rikki's incredulous look, Jade continued. "You have been around mated couples before. You know how hard it is to stay apart. Now, I don't know a lot about this because I was stuck in that place in the middle of the dessert most of my life, but I have seen things since I have been here. The biggest thing is Chase and my mother."

Rikki gasped and her eyes widened. "Exactly," Jade said. "They have been fighting the mating bond since last April. Nine months. Now just imagine how your mate feels after all these years."

"Not only that," Doc Josie interjected, "but you are so young, Rikki. Jeremiah is an older shifter.

I would say just from things I know of him that he is probably 120 to 150 years old." As Rikki's eyes widened, Josie laughed. "I know that seems really old in human years, but in shifter years it's not. I believe Jeremiah is under the impression that you are young and need to live some before being tied to him. Plus, after all of this time, he is probably afraid he will hurt you when you bond. And above all else, he will want you to be safe."

"So he is staying away from me because he thinks I'm too young and he's worried he might hurt me?" Rikki asked, narrowing her eyes. When both Jade and Josie nodded, Rikki stood up, her hands on her hips. "Well that's a bunch of bullshit," she snapped.

Standing up and stepping back in surprise, Jade questioned, "What do you mean?"

"Shit, I may be young, but I have been through more than most people. I've served two tours in the army. Hell, I'm a damn sniper. I kill low lifes for a living. Not only that, but Jeremiah would never hurt me. I may not know a lot about shifters, but I do know mates do not ever physically hurt one another. If he thinks he is staying away from me because of idiotic reasons like that, then he better think again." Shaking her head, Rikki stalked to the door, "Let me know when Trace wakes up. I will be in the waiting room."

Doc Josie laughed softly as the door shut behind Rikki. "Jeremiah Black better watch out. He's definitely met his match in that one."

Opening the medical chart she held, Josie set it on the table beside Trace's bed. Taking hold of the covers, she started to pull them down. At Jade's growl of displeasure, the doctor stopped. "Jade, I'm a doctor. I need to look Trace over to assess the damage that's been done from his time in captivity."

Ashamed, Jade moved to the other side of the bed, reaching for Trace's hand. "I'm sorry. I know that, it's just…"

"I understand," Josie smiled gently. "I've been in your shoes. Until you are fully bonded, the need to hurt any other woman that comes near your man will be there. Just remember, he is yours, Jade. No one can take him from you."

Smiling tremulously, Jade whispered, "I know. It's just hard to believe he's here." Clearing her throat, Jade told Josie, "He has a fever, Doc. I didn't know shifters could get fevers."

"It's because of everything he's been through," Josie responded as she gently probed the bruising around his chest. "Being starved and tortured for so long is hard on a body. And even though Trace heals faster because he is a shifter, a body can only take so much."

As the doctor continued her exam, Jade fought to control herself at the sight of another woman's hands on Trace. In her mind she knew it was for medical purposes only, but after being separated from Trace for so long, it was hard to control her wolf who just saw another woman's hands on her mate.

After several minutes, the doctor pulled the covers back over Trace and reached for her medical chart to jot some notes down. "I am going to give him an antibiotic right now to fight the infection he has. We need to get some food down him as soon as possible, too. It will really help once he is able to shift into his panther form." Looking at Jade she said, "I'm not going to lie, Jade. Trace has been through a lot. There is scarring on his legs that will always be there. When he shifts it will help his infection and all of the bruising, along with most of the wounds, but they seemed to have focused on his legs the most. He will eventually be able to walk normally again, but it won't be an overnight thing."

Josie went to the window and pulled the curtains shut. "You both need some rest, Jade. Try and sleep for a few hours."

"Wait," Jade called out as the doctor went to leave. "What about Gypsy and her sister? How are they?"

Shaking her head sadly, Josie told her, "Not good, Jade. Not good." Watching her go, Jade felt torn. She wanted to be with Trace, but Gypsy and Sari were alone. Trace was sleeping, and Jade knew when he woke up he would want to know exactly what was going on with them. Rubbing her eyes tiredly, Jade decided she better go look in on them herself.

After checking one more time to make sure Trace was still asleep, Jade left the room and went to search for Gypsy. She found her in the next room. Quietly making her way to the bed, Jade gasped at the sight of the small, frail woman in front of her. Gypsy lay on the bed, her covers up to her chin. Her beautiful dark hair fanned out on the pillow around her. There were several bruises marring her delicate features, and one arm lay on top of the blankets covered with a cast. There were stitches on the underside of her chin and more on her other arm.

"I did what I could for her," Doc Josie said from the doorway. "She has a long road ahead of her. I gave her morphine for the pain, and she will be sleeping for a while." Motioning into the hall, Josie huffed, "Come on, I will show you Sari since I see you are just as stubborn as your mother and won't go back to Trace until you have checked on them both."

Taking one last look at the woman who had spent the past few months in hell with Trace, caring for him and pushing him to fight, Jade whispered, "Thank you so much for what you did for my mate. I don't know if Trace would have made it without you there. I will be back, Gypsy. I'm going to check on Sari for you now, but I will be back later, I promise."

Jade missed the lone tear that slid down Gypsy's face as she left the room. Following the doctor across the hall, Jade stopped just inside the door. The young girl lying in the bed was stunning. She was blonde where Gypsy was brunette. Her skin was lighter, but otherwise they were very similar. The poor girl was covered in bruises, as well.

"She was pregnant," Josie said quietly. "When that bastard beat the hell out of her the last time, he kicked her repeatedly in the stomach and ended up killing the baby. She wasn't very far along. My guess is that she didn't even know she was pregnant. But when she wakes up, I will have to tell her."

"She's just a child herself," Jade whispered, tears filling her eyes. Moving to the chair by the bed, Jade sat down. "I will stay with her," she said as she put the footrest out and leaned the chair back. "I can rest here."

"What about Trace?" Josie asked softly from the doorway.

"This is where I am needed," Jade responded, closing her eyes and dismissing the doctor. Sari was terrified, she had been through so much and was about to endure more anguish. As much as she wanted to be with Trace, Jade would not leave the child to wake up alone.

~

Feeling a presence near her, Jade sprang out of the chair with her Glock pulled and ready. "Easy, Jade," she heard Angel murmur. "It's just me."

Shit, she'd been dreaming about something she'd gone through several years ago while being held by the General. Jinx tried to rebel once when Jade was just a child. He only made that mistake once. When it happened, the General brought Jinx to the facility in Arizona and proceeded to hold a gun to Jade's head. The General told Jinx if he ever defied him again, Jade would be dead. Unfortunately, Angel picked a bad time to surprise Jade, as she was reliving the nightmare, and almost got herself shot. "I'm sorry," Jade said quietly as she slid her Glock back in its holster. "Bad memories."

Not responding, Angel walked past her to the bed. Jade was shocked at the amount of pain she was feeling from Angel. Normally Angel held all of her emotions tightly bound and hidden from everyone. Tonight was different. Something had happened. Before she could try and help, Angel growled, "Don't even think about it. These are my feelings. I want them. I need to feel them so I remember why I have to stay strong."

Sighing deeply, Jade said, "I'm going to check on Trace."

"You can stay with him," Angel responded. "I will be here for Sari."

"She's going to need someone when she wakes up," Jade murmured. "We need to make sure she isn't left alone."

When Jade went to leave she heard Angel say, "We will talk about what just happened, Jade. Not tonight, but we will talk." Jade left quietly without responding.

Chapter 13

When Trace finally opened his eyes the next afternoon, he was feeling much better. His legs still hurt like a bitch, but the pain in his arms and chest had receded and he was starving. Not only that, but he had to find the restroom now. Throwing back the covers, he frowned when he realized he didn't have any clothes on. The towel from the night before was still around his hips, and his dick hardened immediately when he remembered the feel of Jade's soft, pink lips surrounding it.

Swinging his legs off the bed, Trace shakily pushed himself to a standing position. The trip to the bathroom was slow, but he was happy he made it without help. Finding a tray of food waiting when he returned from the bathroom, he sat in the chair and quickly demolished it. When he was done, he decided it was time to find his mate. Looking in the closet, he found some scrubs that he put on. They were snug, but would work. Leaving the room, he ignored the looks from the concerned nurses and slowly made his way in the direction of Jade's addicting, sweet scent.

When he reached the front lobby, he saw her in the waiting area. The sight of her standing next to an unknown male, and the scent of her nervousness, brought his cat to the surface. Before Trace could fight it, he was shifted and slowly stalking his prey with a low rumble in his throat.

"Get back," he heard a voice say. "Back slowly away from Jade now, River." When the man turned and saw Trace, he held his hands out to the side and started to move back. Bounding swiftly into the room, Trace slid to a stop in front of Jade and roared menacingly at the other male. Baring his fangs, he growled, a low rumble deep in his chest.

Feeling soft fingers gently stroking his thick, black fur, Trace backed into Jade's legs, but refused to turn away from the threat in front of him. Jade knelt beside him and slipped her arms around his neck, nuzzling close. "It's okay, Trace," she assured him. "I'm okay. This is River. He's one of Chase's enforcers. He was just coming to check on his friend that was hurt on patrol earlier."

Snarling at River one last time, Trace buried his nose into Jade's neck and purred. He still considered River a threat; all males were a threat until he claimed Jade. But Trace had realized that the room was filled with his teammates, so for now he wasn't worried.

"Well," Angel interrupted, "Since you seem to be doing better, Trace, we need to have a meeting.

Take Jade back to your room with you and we will be there in five minutes."

With one last glare at River, Trace nudged Jade to his room. Once the door was closed behind them, Trace shifted and pushed Jade up against it crushing his lips to hers. Sliding past her lips at her shocked gasp, he tangled his tongue with hers, holding his body tightly against her. He wanted to strip her right then and make her his, but the sound of footsteps heading in their direction made him pull back. That dazed, sultry expression on her face was for him, and only him. After kissing her one more time, Trace wrapped an arm tightly around her waist. Tugging gently, he maneuvered her to the bed. Sliding in, he scooted over and tugged her in beside him. He needed her close, wanted her body next to his. Jade pulled the covers up over them, and snuggled into him just as the door opened and Angel walked in, followed by the rest of the team. Using the remote on the side of the bed, Trace raised the bed into a sitting position.

"Nice to have you back, T," Rikki said as she moved up to stand beside Jade. "It's sucked doing my job and yours." Trace chuckled, bumping fists with her. He knew Rikki was joking. It was her way of telling him she had missed him.

Trace let a small grin steal over his face as he greeted the rest of his team. He took in Ryker, Storm, and Flame before glancing at Angel in question. "They are with us now," she said. "A part of RARE. Flame's trained hard and has earned her place. Ryker and Storm left the Shifter Council to come work with us. That's a story for another time. Right now, we have something important to discuss."

Taking in the seriousness of Angel's gaze, Trace stilled. Somehow he knew whatever was wrong had to do with him, and it was bad. Stepping closer to him, Angel said, "Trace, everyone in this room is your family. We would give our lives for you. And because we are family, your mother and sister are our family, too."

Trace tightened his arm around Jade, but didn't respond. "Sophia and Starr are in trouble, Trace," Angel continued. "Sari heard Perez tell someone that he has a lead on them. Jaxson has been trying to track them down, but hasn't been able to yet. We have to get to them before your father does. You need to tell us where you have them hidden."

A sense of urgency hitting him at the thought of his mother and sister being found by Perez had Trace moving to get out of bed. "Stop Trace," Angel commanded. "You are in no condition to go anywhere right now." Sitting on the edge of the bed, Trace clenched his hands tightly into fists, fear and anger pouring through him.

Feeling Jade's hand running soothingly up and down his back, Trace took a deep breath fighting the urge to leave and find his family. They were in danger, but Angel was right. He could hardly walk down the hall right now. There was no way he was going to save them on his own. At this point, he would be more of a hindrance on a mission than a help. But dammit, they were *his* family.

Looking at Angel, he nodded and slid back under the covers, pulling Jade close again to calm his emotions. "Let us help, T," Rikki said softly. "You would do it for us."

"I promised them I would always keep them safe," he rasped, his heart pounding in fear. "They were there for me when no one else was. My mom was my moon, and my sister my star." Glancing around the room, Trace said, "My father is an animal. A fucking animal. I could kill him with my bare hands for the things he did to my mother alone. But you add in what he did to my sister…" Shaking his head, Trace leaned back against the bed shutting his eyes tightly.

"We will find them, Trace," Angel promised him. "We will find them and bring them home."

"It won't matter," Trace sighed. "Until that bastard is eliminated, he will always look for them. Perez is transfixed on my mother for some reason.

He will do everything in his power to have her again. I've been hiding them for years, changing the places at least every six months. I've been lucky until now."

"Tell me where, Trace," Jaxson said as he took out his laptop and quickly turned it on. "We'll get to them before he does."

Taking a deep breath, Trace tightened his grip on Jade and said, "There in Taos, New Mexico," he admitted reluctantly.

Jaxson raised an eyebrow, "Are you serious? That's like a five hour drive from here."

Shrugging, Trace said, "I know. Mom said she wanted to be closer to me. And I thought it would be easier to keep them safe if they were."

After Jaxson pulled up the exact location of Trace's family, RARE started making plans. It was a five hour drive, but they were flying. "I'm going," Trace insisted. "They won't know they can trust you. They'll get scared and run."

Eyeing him, Angel finally nodded. "Fine, you go. But you let me know if you think you can't make it at any time, Trace. I won't allow you to screw up this mission."

"I will," Trace promised. And he would. There was no way he was going to mess up a mission this important.

"Ok, we leave in an hour. I need to get this past the Doc, Trace," Angel warned.

"I don't give a shit what she says," Trace snarled. "I'm going."

Glancing over at the low growl that escaped Ryker, Angel laughed. "You better show Ryker's mate some respect, Trace."

"That's right," Doc Josie said as she walked in the room, stopping to kiss a pissed off Ryker, before smiling at Trace. "Ryker and I mated last month, Trace. Now, what's going on here that the whole RARE team is crammed into your room?"

"We're leaving on another mission, Josie," Ryker said as he tugged her into his arms. Resting his chin on her head, he told her, "It's very important that Trace comes with us. We won't let him do too much, but the people we are going to save only know him. If he isn't there, they could be scared off. If they are found by the wrong person, he'll kill them."

"Well," Josie drawled as she pulled away from Ryker and walked over to Trace, "wasn't that a lot of nothing you just told me."

When she went to pull down the covers so she could look at Trace's chest, he grabbed her wrist. Ignoring Ryker's growl of warning, Trace said, "My mother and sister are in danger, Doc. My father is hunting them right now and if we don't get to them first, he will kill them."

"Now see," Josie said as she gently tugged her wrist out of his grasp, "that wasn't so hard was it? I want you to shift back into your panther for as long as possible. It will help you heal faster. No fighting. You get in, get your family and get out. Let everyone else do the hard part. If you need me when you get back, I will be here."

"Thanks Doc," Trace responded gratefully. "No offense, but I hope I don't need ya." Josie laughed as she left the room.

"Get ready people," Angel said as she walked toward the door, "be ready to leave here in an hour. Wheels up in an hour and a half. Trace, I want you in your panther form until the damn plane lands, you feel me?" At Trace's nod, Angel left with the rest of the group following. When Phoenix reached the door, he glanced back with a wink and locked it on his way out.

The minute they were gone, Trace tilted Jade's head up to his, taking her mouth in a deep kiss. Her lips parted on a moan, granting him entrance, and he took full advantage of it. Grabbing the remote, he put the bed back down so it laid flat and then covered Jade's body with his own. Holding her head between his hands, he assaulted her mouth while grinding his hips into her thigh, the friction against his dick driving him wild. "I need you, Jade," he groaned. "I didn't want to take you like this. Not in the hospital. I wanted our first time to be special with candles, flowers, wine. But I can't wait any longer. I'm going fucking crazy."

Moaning, Jade arched into him gasping, "I don't need all of that, Trace. I just need you. Take me."

That was all Trace needed to hear. Leaning back, he pulled Jade's shirt up over her head quickly, baring her soft, lily white skin to his gaze. Unhooking her bra, he slipped it off before cupping her perfect breast in the palm of his hand. He loved the contrast of her light skin against the darkness of his own. It was sexy as hell. And her light pink nipples were begging for his mouth. Lowering his head, he tasted her nipple, teasing it with his tongue before sucking it into his mouth. He sucked harder at her soft cry of pleasure, then releasing her breast, he placed soft kisses down the silky skin on her belly.

Reaching between them, he unbuttoned her pants and slid them down, removing them from her legs and tossing them carelessly to the floor.

Hooking his fingers in the waistband of her panties, he slowly slipped them down her long, beautiful legs. He couldn't wait to have them wrapped around him soon.

Leaning down, Trace slowly kissed and nibbled his way from Jade's ankle up her leg, to the inside of her thigh. "Oh God," Jade cried out as he nuzzled her mound before spreading her lips and licking up to her clit. Taking her clit into his mouth, he gently tugged on it before stroking it with his tongue. As Jade's moans grew louder, Trace slipped a finger inside her and moved his tongue faster. Jade screamed as she came just moments later.

Not willing to wait any longer, Trace slid up Jade's body and taking hold of his aching cock, he slowly started to push inside her. He froze at Jade's slight grunt of discomfort. Oh shit, he thought as he tried to pull out. Jade grabbed hold of his ass and pushed up hard against him, sinking him deeply inside her hot, moist heat in one thrust. Forcing himself to stay still while Jade adjusted to him being inside her, he sucked in a ragged breath as he buried his face in her neck. His cat was urging him to hurry, to bite and claim his mate. But Trace refused to hurt Jade. He should have realized she was innocent, but he'd been thinking mostly with his dick. He waited until he felt her slowly start to rotate her hips. Groaning at the fire shooting up his spine, he fought the desire to pound into her.

Finally, unable to hold back, Trace pushed deeper into Jade and then slowly pulled back out. Shaking, sweat beading up on his forehead, he pushed in again, and then again and again. Jade panted softly in his ear, then he heard her whisper, "Harder." Grabbing hold of her hair, he fisted it in his hand and held her head still while he took her mouth with his. As he thrust his tongue in and out of her mouth, he moved harder and faster into Jade. Yanking her mouth away, Jade cried, "More, Trace. I need more."

Trace snarled as he pounded into her. Reaching between them, he flicked her clit with his thumb and she screamed as she came, squeezing his dick tightly. Trace roared loudly and sank his fangs into her shoulder, claiming her as he came. As he licked the puncture wounds closed, he felt Jade's fangs sink deep into his shoulder and he came again on another roar.

"Mine," he whispered as he licked his claiming bite. "Mine."

"Always," Jade promised as she licked at her own mating bite.

Rolling over, Trace pulled Jade onto his chest and gently stroked her hair. Softly kissing the top of her head, Trace whispered, "You are everything to me, Jade. No matter what may happen in the future, I promise to always care for you and cherish you. I will protect you above all else. I love you, my mate."

As he drifted into sleep, Trace didn't notice the guilty look on Jade's face. He didn't feel her leave the bed or see her get dressed and slip quietly from the room. But he did notice her absence when he woke twenty minutes later, alone in the bed where he'd just claimed his mate.

Chapter 14

Running through the woods as fast as she could, Jade screamed loudly into the cold, quiet evening. Rage consumed her as guilt swamped her. Her mate trusted her, he said he loved her. But there were things he didn't know about her. Things she kept hidden from the world. Jade wanted to share everything with Trace, but there was so much to consider. Most importantly, Jinx.

Stopping, Jade dropped to her knees on the cold, damp ground. Ignoring the wetness seeping into her jeans, she wrapped her arms tightly around herself and sobbed. She was mad as hell and her heart was breaking. She didn't want to begin her mating with lies. God, why hadn't she told him everything before they'd bonded? What if he didn't want her when he realized who she really was?

Hearing a noise behind her, Jade froze. Baring her teeth on a snarl, she turned, but relaxed when she saw Chase. Walking past her, he moved to sit on a log a few feet away. "Come here, little one," he said quietly, patting the space next to him. Slowly, Jade stood up and walked over, taking a seat beside him.

"I can feel your pain," he said as he stared into the darkening woods. "You want to talk about it?"

Jade hesitated as she wiped the tears from her cheeks. She'd never had an Alpha. She knew an Alpha took care of his pack, putting them above everything else. He was there to both protect and comfort them. Most wolves ran in packs, but Jade and Jinx only had each other. She guessed you could call Jinx her Alpha, although she didn't think of him in that way. To her, he was her brother.

"Talk to me, Jade," Chase demanded softly. "Let me help."

She was supposed to be a warrior. That's what Jinx trained her for. But right now she felt like a child, so lost and scared. "It's always just been me and Jinx," Jade whispered. "The two of us against the world. I've never had an Alpha."

"You have Angel now," Chase reminded her as he continued to scan the area around them. "She's a powerful Alpha."

"Angel's my mother, not my Alpha," Jade stated. "I don't want her as my Alpha." Clasping her hands tightly together, Jade whispered hesitantly, "But I would like you to be, I think."

Reaching over, Chase covered her shaking hands with his. "Then I will be," he said. Suddenly

Jade felt Chase pushing his power into her, helping to calm her and take away some of the fear. Closing her eyes, she soaked it in, wondering if this was what others felt like when she helped them.

"Now, as Alpha it is my honor and privilege to take care of my pack and help them with anything and everything they need. Talk to me, Jade. Let me help you."

When Jade didn't respond, Chase asked, "Does this have anything to do with your mating?"

Jade gulped and stared at her feet as Chase waited patiently for a response. Finally, raising her head and looking her new Alpha directly in the eyes, Jade told him, "Trace trusts me, Chase. He says he loves me, but he doesn't know the real me. The one I have to keep hidden from everyone. He sees a sweet, innocent Omega wolf. I haven't been sweet and innocent since I was eight years old and made my first kill. And I am definitely not an Omega wolf. The person he loves…that's not me."

"We all have our secrets, Jade," Chase said. "Some secrets are worse than others. But tell me something. Do you really think Trace would love you any less if he knew yours?" When Jade would have responded, Chase held up a hand. "Think about this. In a year, where do you want to be, Jade? With a mate that loves you and would do anything for you…or alone? Talk to him. Let him decide how he feels about it, about you. But give him the chance to make his own decision. That's very important."

Holding back her tears and fear of losing her mate, Jade nodded. "I know you're right. But I also have to think of my brother. Some of my secrets include him."

"Jinx will want you to be happy," Chase promised. "And you can trust Trace. Whatever you tell him will go no further."

"I know," Jade whispered. "I trust him with my life."

"And you can trust him with your brother's," Chase said softly. "One more thing, Jade, you might want to consider talking to your mother about all of this, too. Angel will not judge you. She's lived without you for 20 years. All she wants is the chance to love you and have that love returned. There isn't anything that woman wouldn't do for you and Jinx, Jade. That goes for me, too."

Standing, Chase held out his hand to her. "Let's go. I have a feeling your mate is getting restless. I know you are supposed to be leaving soon to get his family."

Gasping, Jade jumped up quickly. "Oh no! We need to hurry!" Running back to the hospital,

Chase on her heels, Jade prayed RARE had waited for her. She couldn't believe she'd forgotten about Trace's family. What kind of mate was she?

The kind that will love unconditionally, as will he, Jinx's voice whispered into her mind. *Your Alpha is right, sis. All I want is for you to be happy. Trust your mate. Tell him everything.*

Not slowing her pace, Jade asked hesitantly, *Are you sure?*

Yes, was Jinx's quick response. *It's time you tell Angel, too.*

Will you come talk to them with me? She asked. *I don't know if I can do it on my own.*

You are stronger than you think, Jade. Jinx said, the pride evident in his voice. *But you won't be on your own. You will never have to do anything on your own again, sis. If I can't be there, your Alpha, Angel and Trace will be. You are finally safe.*

There was silence for a moment as Jade let what Jinx said sink in. She was safe. She was free. And as long as Trace fully accepted her for who she was, she was loved.

When will you be safe, Jinx? she asked softly.

As soon as I bring that bastard down, Jinx growled. D*on't worry about me, Jade. I've got this. You go to your mate. Be happy.*

As they neared the hospital, Trace stepped through the front entrance, a dark scowl on his face. The RARE team members waited by two black SUV's near the building. Skidding to a stop in front of the hospital steps, Jade reached back and grabbed Chase's hand for courage. Feeling his power flowing through her, she looked up into her mate's pissed off gaze. He glanced down to where Jade clasped Chase's hand and then back up to her eyes, and Jade smiled, letting her love show in her gaze. Shoring up her courage, reminding herself she was free to live her life now, she said softly, "I love you, too, my mate."

Trace was down the stairs pulling Jade into his arms in the next instant, her face buried in his neck. Breathing deeply, she inhaled his dark, spicy scent that was now mixed with her own. She felt the huge shudder run through his body as she clung to him. *You will tell me why you left me,* Trace demanded roughly.

Trembling, Jade said, *I will. Just please, promise me you will still love me.*

Leaning back, Trace tilted her head up, gazing into her eyes. *I will always love you, Jade,* he vowed. *Nothing will ever take you from me.*

Smiling again, Jade kissed him softly on the lips before saying out loud, "Let's go get your family. Then, when we get back, we will talk." Glancing at Chase she whispered, "Thank you for everything, Alpha."

At Angel's gasp of surprise, Chase stepped forward and rested a hand on Jade's shoulder. "I will be here if you need me, Jade." Nodding to the others, he walked up the hospital steps and through the doors.

"Chase is your Alpha now?" Angel questioned with a slight note of disbelief and a hint of jealousy in her tone.

"Yes," Jade responded quietly. "I want an Alpha. My wolf needs one." At the hurt expression on Angel's face that she quickly masked, Jade went on, "I don't need you to be my Alpha, Angel. I need you to be my mother."

A slow smile spread across Angel's face before she said, "I have always been your mother, Jade. And I have always loved you. Nothing will change that."

"Sorry to interrupt," Rikki interjected, "but we need to beat feet. There's another family reunion on our list tonight. And all this mushy crap is giving me a headache."

"She's right," Angel agreed. "We need to get going." Turning to Trace she narrowed her eyes. "Why haven't you shifted?"

Ignoring her, Trace wrapped an arm around Jade's waist and walked with her to one of the SUVs. Opening the middle door on the passenger side, Trace helped Jade in and then turned to the team. "Let's do this," he growled before sliding in beside Jade and pulling the door shut.

Leaning her head against Trace's shoulder, Jade closed her eyes tiredly. It had been so long since she'd slept more than four hours at a time. Feeling Trace's arm slide around her, she snuggled into his side. She needed some rest before the mission or she wouldn't be at full strength. Jade let herself drift off to sleep in the comfort of her mate's arms, knowing that for once in her life she was truly safe.

Chapter 15

When Jade finally opened her eyes again, they had already boarded the plane and were in the air. Sitting up and looking around in confusion, she saw she was in the back of the jet on the floor. Trace lay next to her in cat form, his midnight black fur shining. "Trace didn't want to wake you when we got to the hangar," Rikki said from beside them in her chair. "Stubborn ass insisted on carrying you on the plane himself. Angel made him shift after he laid you down. The doc says it will help speed the healing process along."

Running a hand through her tangled hair, Jade sighed. "If I would have stayed with him instead of running off because I got scared, he would have shifted a long time ago," she admitted. Placing a hand on Trace, she slid her fingers through his thick fur.

"So," Rikki began reluctantly. "Can I ask you something?"

"Of course," Jade responded absently, her attention on Trace.

"I know there are things you aren't telling us, hell we all know it," Rikki laughed softly. "Which is fine, Jade. Unless you are hiding something that could affect a mission we are on, I really don't give a shit."

"I would never put the team in danger," Jade snapped, anger in her voice.

"Good," Rikki said. "So, although I can tell you have a gentle nature and like to help others when they are upset or in pain, I know you aren't an Omega wolf. I also know you would have us believe you were if you could."

Jade glanced down guilty, then back up at Rikki. Holding her head high, she said, "Not anymore. I'm not hiding who I am anymore. I decided when we went to get Trace in Colombia that I was done playing the Omega wolf card. And when I spoke with Jinx recently, he told me I am finally free to be whoever I want to be," Tightening her grip in Trace's fur, she said, "He said I'm finally safe. That Trace, Chase and Angel will protect me when Jinx can't."

"And he's right," Nico said from his seat two seats up. Turning around to face them, he told Jade, "Your mom, your Alpha and your mate will always keep you safe. But they aren't the only ones, Jade. The rest of us will, too. You are Angel's daughter, a part of this family. We protect what's ours."

Gazing at the faces around her, Jade smiled gratefully, before her smile dimmed. "But what about Jinx?" she whispered. "Who will keep him safe?"

"We will," Angel promised, from her position at the front of the plane. "We will help him take down the General, Jade. And then we will bring your brother home."

Trace purred deeply, nudging her thigh with his nose. Smiling down at him, she gently stroked his neck. "So, Rikki, what was your question?" she asked, changing the subject, as she continued running her hands over the beautiful black panther lying next to her.

"I know you can fight, Jade," Rikki said. "No matter how hard you tried to hide it, I always knew you could fight and shoot. I don't, however, get the impression you enjoy it. If feels more like you do it because you have to, not because you want to."

Nodding her head in agreement, Jade said, "Jinx taught me to fight and shoot." Glancing over at her mate she admitted softly, "He taught me to kill. I can kill a man several different ways. And I have."

"Exactly," Rikki exclaimed. "I saw it. I accidentally touched your coat one day without my gloves. I promise you it wasn't on purpose, but it happened. I saw you dressed in this skimpy little teddy thing. You were in a hotel room with some sleaze ball. The guy said something to you. You smiled at him, and then slipped a knife out from under a pillow and slit his throat."

At the threatening rumble in Trace's throat, Jade whispered into his mind, *I promise I didn't sleep with him, Trace.*

The rumbling slowly stopped and then he growled, *I know you didn't, baby. A man can tell when he's a woman's first. I just don't like the thought of anyone else seeing you naked.*

"My question," Rikki continued, unaware of the discussion going on between Trace and Jade, "is if you are capable of something like that, then why did you let that sick bastard kick your ass back in May? You almost died. You could have taken him!"

Trace's head snapped up and he rose slowly. Baring his teeth, he let out a powerful roar. "Oh shit," Rikki said, her eyes going wide. "Trace didn't know what happened?"

"No," Angel said as she slowly made her way back to a very pissed off cat shifter. "I didn't tell him because he didn't need the distraction."

Trace crouched low, his whole body vibrating with rage, ready to spring at Angel. Jade moved quickly, wrapping her arms around his neck and trying to push him back. "It's ok, Trace. I'm fine. It never should have happened in the first place. But it wasn't anyone's fault but my own."

Shifting quickly out of his cat, Trace pulled Jade into his lap, holding her tightly against him. "That was not your choice to make, Angel," he growled. "Jade is my mate, dammit. I should have been here for her."

"Your place at the time was tracking down your father," Angel insisted, glaring at him, her hands on her hips. "I was here for Jade."

"Actually, Trace is right," Jade interjected coldly. "His place was with me. You should have contacted him. But now is not the time to debate this. You need to back away and let him calm down."

Turning to Rikki as Angel stubbornly refused to move, Jade said, "To answer your question, Rikki, I didn't kick his ass because there were too many emotions being thrown in my direction and I couldn't keep them locked out. The man was full of hate and anger. The children were terrified, the women were scared for the children. It was all too much. Normally I can block out most emotions, but this time they consumed me and I lost my focus. Jinx tried to help, but there was nothing he could do. I was too far gone."

"I don't understand," Rikki said in confusion. "What do you mean when you say you couldn't block them out? Did you connect with them like Angel does? Were you inside their minds?"

Shaking her head, Jade said, "No. I do have that ability, but I'm also an empath. A very strong empath. I can sense feelings and emotions in everyone, sometimes from a great distance. That's how I am able to help calm others. With my empathic gift. I can also hear people's thoughts. Normally I can block them out like Jinx taught me, but sometimes the feelings overwhelm me."

"How the hell do you function like that?" Flame asked incredulously. "I would go crazy if I had to know what others were thinking or feeling all of the time."

"I don't know any different," Jade said shrugging. "I've always been like this."

"Always?" Angel asked softly.

"Yes," Jade said glancing over at her mother. "Always."

"So all of the pain I felt when you were so young?"

"I felt it all as well," Jade confirmed. "Your grief when you thought Dad betrayed you. The pain you felt daily over losing Jinx. I felt it all from a very young age."

"But you never said anything," Angel whispered, clutching tightly to the seat beside her. "I could have hidden it from you somehow."

"I didn't know what was happening to me back then. I kept it from you because you were always so sad, and I didn't want to make it worse. I was so young, I just thought I was sick. Jinx is the one that explained it to me."

"We're here," Jaxson yelled from the front of the plane. "Buckle up. We're getting some turbulence. Landing in two minutes."

As Angel moved back to her seat and buckled in, Trace asked softly, "When you kill, do you feel any backlash?"

"Yes," Jade admitted. "It's painful. But I'm learning how to suppress it so it's not as bad as it was at first."

"Are these some of the things you've been afraid to tell me, Jade?" Trace questioned as he brushed a piece of hair back behind her ear.

"Yes," Jade admitted as she leaned forward and rested her head on his chest. "I'm a trained killer. But not by the General. He has no idea what I can do. Jinx trained me. He said if he was ever able to get me away from the General, then he knew I would stand a fighting chance on my own."

"We are all trained killers," Rikki said softly. "All deadly in our own right." Jade's eyes widened as she lifted her head to look at Rikki.

"Exactly," Trace agreed. "You were stuck in hell, Jade. You did what you had to do to survive. I am so damn proud of you."

"But I killed by the General's orders," Jade said. "They were Jinx's orders, but I carried them out in my training."

"Have you ever killed an innocent?" Phoenix asked. "Have you ever put a bullet in someone that didn't deserve to die?

"Well, no," Jade admitted. "They had all wronged the General in some way, but the people that back him or run in his circles are into illegal drug trafficking and selling women. Things like that."

"Then, I for one am glad you sliced and diced that bastard," Phoenix said with a shrug. "I don't care if you were trained by the devil himself. As long as you don't go after the innocent, you are golden in my book."

Jade thought about what they said as the plane touched ground. They were right. Every person on that plane was trained to not only protect, but to kill when needed. In their eyes, all of her killings were justified. And Trace was proud of her; her heart swelled with that knowledge.

Waiting for Trace to get dressed while everyone disembarked from the plane, Jade did something she hadn't done since she was a child. She prayed. She prayed their mission would go smoothly. She prayed for Gypsy and Sari. And she prayed for Jinx. Because if she could find her way away from the General and into the arms of someone like Trace, maybe Jinx would too.

Chapter 16

Moving quickly through the small housing development where Trace had hidden Sophia and Starr for the past year, RARE fanned out making sure to stay in the shadows. Trace was managing to stay with the team, but it was a fight to keep up. His entire body hurt like crazy, but he fought through the pain. His mother and sister needed him.

Slow up, Angel ordered. *Something's off.* The team cautiously moved closer, slowly clearing the area around the house they were silently stalking. When they had formed a barrier around the house a number of yards out, Angel said, *Find a home Rikki and Storm. Let me know what you see.* She'd known it was useless trying to keep Trace from his family, so Angel was allowing him to infiltrate with them this time instead of finding a place to hide with his sniper rifle. However, she'd warned him that if he felt the need to draw back at any time, he damn well better do it. Like that was going to happen, Trace huffed to himself.

The team stilled as they waited for Rikki and Storm to report. *I've got one woman, two men. They're in the living room, front part of the house,* Rikki quietly responded from her position on the south side of the house.

One woman, one man, Storm replied. *Second floor, far room on the east side. She's on her knees on the floor. Asshole has a gun to her head.*

Looks like they are waiting for something, boss, Rikki said. *Think that's us?*

I know it is, Angel growled. *Well, let's give them what they're waiting for.* As Angel started issuing orders, the team quickly complied. *Jaxson, Ryker, Flame, you take the second floor. Take that bastard out if you can. If you can't get to him, have Storm take the shot. Phoenix, wire the place to blow. I don't want to leave bodies, and there will definitely be two by the sounds of it. The rest of you are with me. We go in after we know the others made it.*

Trace watched as Jaxson, Ryker and Flame shimmied up the house using whatever means they could find. *It has to be Starr upstairs,* he said quietly. *If Perez found my mother, he won't let her out of his sight. And he won't be without at least one body guard.* Eyes narrowing, he muttered, *I could be wrong, but I swear that son of a bitch, Titus, knows I'm a shifter. It comes from my mom's side of the family, but we have always kept it a secret from my father.*

We're in boss, Flame murmured through their link. *But you better hurry. I think we might have a problem.*

Talk to me, Angel demanded as she slipped through a window in one of the back rooms, Trace and Jade right behind her.

Starr is pissed. I think she's about to make a move. Jaxson said. *I'm unable to get her attention.*

Shit, Trace growled, *my sister has a temper. She's not trained though. She's gonna get herself killed.*

No she's not, Jaxson promised. *I got your sister, T. You get your mom.*

Even though it was hard to place his trust in anyone, Trace knew Jaxson would do everything in his power to keep Starr safe. Pulling his Glock from his side holster, Trace silently followed Angel down the hall, stopping when he heard his father's voice. "Oh, see, that's where you are wrong, Sophia. My son will be here soon. And when he gets here, I am going to do what I should have done when I had the little prick in my Dungeon. I'm going to put a bullet between his eyes. No one steals from me!"

Peering around the corner Trace saw a guard standing on the far side of the room, his back to a wall. Trace's mother was sitting on the couch, Perez towering over her. "I haven't seen Trace in over a year, Philip," she insisted. "Wait," she paused, "What do you mean you had him in your Dungeon?"

Laughing cruelly, Perez moved to stand in front of her. "I caught your precious son, bitch. He was in the jungle killing off my men. But I caught him. The little shit never knew what torture was until Titus got a hold of him."

"You have Trace?" Sophia whispered, her eyes filling with tears. "You hurt my son?" she questioned, her voice rising.

"I should have killed him," Perez sneered, "but I was hoping he would turn on you and give up your location. No matter what Titus did to him, he refused to talk. Funny thing is, Sophia, he seemed to be feeling much better just a few short days after each session with Titus. Any idea why that might be, my bitch of a wife?"

Standing, Sophia placed her hands on her hips, her body trembling in outrage. Ignoring his question she demanded, "Where is my son you bastard?"

Trace froze as Perez slapped his mother hard, sending her flying back onto the couch. Before Trace could move, a small white wolf leaped over him, attacking Perez, pushing him back away from Sophia.

Shit! Now Trace! Angel ordered as she entered the living room and went after the guard. Trace snarled and leaped for his father, taking him to the floor. He saw the wolf, his magnificent mate, move to stand in front of his mother, her fangs bared, lip curled on a snarl. She would protect Sophia while Trace ended the bastard that had made his life a living hell.

Turning back to Perez, he yanked him up by the front of his shirt and shoved him against the wall. "You will never hurt my family again, you son of a bitch." Slamming a fist in Perez's face, Trace grunted in satisfaction at the sound of bone breaking. Blood seeped from his nose, but the psychotic grin his father sported never left his face.

Laughing, Perez said, "I know what you are, Trace. I figured it out after I met someone just like you."

Ignoring his mother's gasp, Trace growled, "Who?"

"A prisoner," Perez sneered. "No matter what I did to her, given enough time, she always healed. I thought maybe Gypsy was like her, but it turns out I was wrong. Although, Gypsy was fun to experiment on."

"And just where is this prisoner?" Trace asked incredulously. "The only female prisoner you had when I was there was Gypsy."

Shrugging, Perez laughed again. "I sold her."

"To who?" Angel growled as she made her way to them, the guard's lifeless body left on the floor behind her.

"There's a man looking for people like you," Perez sneered, his gaze going to where Jade stood, her glorious white coat shining brightly in the dimness of the room. "I bet I could get a pretty penny for that one," he said as he watched her hungrily.

Trace's claws sprung from his fingertips, but Angel's voice stopped him before he tore out Perez's throat. "I want a name," she said in a low, deadly voice. Slipping a knife from a sheath on her leg, she moved closer. Placing the tip of it into Perez's jugular she growled, "A name, you sick fuck."

On a slow smile, Perez said, "I don't know his name. All I know is he goes by the General. I sold him Raven last year, although I'm still not sure what that pretty little thing can actually shift in to. No matter what I did to her, the most I saw were some fangs. But, I promised him, Trace." His eyes narrowing, Perez said, "And his men should be here any minute to collect him."

Eyes widening in shock, Angel pulled back with a nod to Trace. Not wasting another second, Trace sliced through Perez's throat with his claws, letting his body slide to the ground. *We need to go. Now!* Angel ordered as she motioned for Trace, Jade and Sophia to follow her quietly. Gently helping his mother off the couch and placing a finger to his lips, he slipped his fingers into Jade's coat, silently thanking her.

I have your sister, Jaxson said. *Damn, she is a wildcat, Trace. Are you sure she isn't a shifter?*

No she's not, and keep your damn hands off her, Trace retorted as he guided his mother out of the living room and back the way they came.

We need to hurry, Angel interjected. *Perez has been working with the General. He knows we're here.*

Let me know when you are all clear, Phoenix said. *I'm ready to light this place up!*

Clear, Ryker and Jaxson responded as Trace was helping his mother out the window. Stepping back, he waited for Jade to jump through, before slipping quickly out himself. *Clear,* he told Phoenix as they ran through the back yard.

Meet back at the vehicles, Angel ordered at the first sound of an explosion.

Scooping his mother up in his arms, Trace raced to where they'd hidden the SUV's. Once there, he gently set her on her feet. "Mom," Starr cried from where she stood by Jaxson. Rushing over, she folded Sophia close, before murmuring, "I'm so glad you're safe."

Looking up to see Trace standing there, Starr pulled away from her mother and moved to stand in front of him. Placing her hands on her hips she spat, "Where the hell have you been? You fucking left us here alone for over a year, Trace. That bastard almost got us! He almost got mom. And where were you?"

A low warning growl slipped from Jade as she stepped in front of Trace. Baring her teeth, she backed closer to Trace, her dark green eyes flashing in anger. "Oh," Starr said snidely, "I see. You left us here while you were out screwing…"

Before she could finish Angel stepped forward and interrupted, "You better rethink what you are going to say right now, Starr. If you insult my daughter, your brother's mate, you will have to deal with me. I don't give a shit who you are."

Turning wide, surprised eyes in Angel's direction, Starr took a step back at the power flowing from the Alpha. "And maybe you should ask your brother where he's been instead of jumping his ass. I'm sure he would much rather have been here looking in on you then sitting chained up in your father's Dungeon getting beaten and tortured. But don't worry, he didn't give up your location. I have no idea how Perez got it, but it wasn't through your loyal brother you are yelling at and ridiculing in front of everyone. I know him and trust him, even if you don't seem to."

Hanging her head in shame, Starr whispered, "When Trace didn't come back, I got scared. We waited and waited. I told Mom we needed to move before we were found, but she insisted on waiting for Trace." Turning to her brother, she apologized softly, "I'm so sorry. In my heart I know you wouldn't just leave us, Trace. But it was easier to believe that than to think about you being caught, or worse, dead."

Pulling Starr close and wrapping his arms around her tightly, Trace whispered, "I understand." Leaning back, he smiled gently, "He's dead, Starr. I killed the bastard. You don't have to worry about him anymore."

As her eyes filled with hope, Angel interjected, "No, but you do need to worry about the General. Let's get going people!"

"Wait," Jaxson said as they started piling into the vehicles. "Where's Rikki and Storm? They should have been here by now."

Pain, there's so much pain, Jade whispered to them, whining softly. *It's Rikki.*

"Get in the SUV, Trace. Take your mother, Starr, Flame, and Jaxson and get the hell out of here!

Get to the plane and get ready to leave as soon as I'm there." Turning quickly, Angel left, Nico, Phoenix and Ryker following quickly behind.

Jaxson slid into the driver's seat and started the vehicle. Flame took the seat next to him, her gun drawn and ready. After urging his mother and Starr into the back, Trace slid into the middle with Jade beside him. Jaxson put the car in gear and headed to the small airport where they'd left the plane. Reaching under the seat, Trace pulled out a pair of sweats and sat them on the seat beside Jade. "Shift," he told her. "We need all guns ready if the General is sniffing around here."

After shifting and quickly pulling on her clothes, Jade pulled out an extra Glock from the back of the seat. Moving to her side of the SUV, she held the gun ready, scanning the area. Seeing the slight tremble in her hand, Trace promised, "It's going to be okay, Jade. Your mom will be back soon."

Turning wide, tear filled eyes in his direction, she whispered, "I'm not worried about my mother, Trace. I'm worried about one of the only true friends I have in this world. I don't think she's going to make it. She's in so much pain and there's so much blood." As Trace watched, Jade seemed to close in on herself. She turned her gaze back to the window beside her, scanning the area furtively.

Reaching over, Trace ran a hand down Jade's back. "Rikki's a fighter, Jade. She will make it." With a small shake of her head, Jade continued looking out the window, not responding.

Chapter 17

Angel picked up her pace as she saw Rikki on the ground below the tree she'd been hiding in. She was lying in a pool of blood, and Storm was nowhere to be found.

Rikki had a tight hold on the side of her neck, her eyes wide with fear. Kneeling beside her, Angel took hold of her free hand. It was bad. It was obvious a bullet had grazed her neck and nicked an artery, causing Rikki to lose a lot of blood. If she were a shifter with the ability to heal more quickly, she would have a fighting chance. But as a human, Angel wasn't sure she would make it.

Nico crouched down beside Rikki, opening the first aid kit he'd brought from the SUV. Grabbing some dressing from the kit, he gently removed Rikki's hand and applied pressure himself. "We need to get her to Doc Josie now," he said as he softly brushed Rikki's hair out of her face.

"Angel," Rikki stuttered as she tried to talk. When Angel tried to tell her not to speak, Rikki frantically started shaking her head.

"Stop," Nico ordered roughly, "You have to stop Rikki. We'll listen."

Eyeing him gratefully, she rasped, "General's men...took Storm." Squeezing her hand tightly, Angel motioned for Ryker and Phoenix to case the area. Unfortunately there was no sign of the General's men or Storm. The burning house was causing a commotion in the neighborhood, and Angel could hear the sound of fire engines getting close. "We have to go," she said as she knelt back down by Rikki.

"What about Storm?" Ryker growled, his bear evident in his voice. Storm was Ryker's best friend. If she was hurt, there would be hell to pay.

"She's gone, Ryker," Angel said. "Right now we need to concentrate on Rikki. We will find Storm. I promise." Looking to Nico she asked, "Can Rikki be moved?"

"Do we have a choice?" Nico shot back. Phoenix stepped forward and gently lifted Rikki in his arms while Nico held tightly to the bandage on her neck. "Why didn't I see this?" Nico asked in despair. "Why didn't I fucking see this?"

Laying a hand on his back, Angel whispered, "It doesn't work like that, Nico. You don't always see everything, and even when you do, it doesn't mean we can change it."

"You can change this," they heard a voice say from the darkness. Angel froze as Jinx stepped out of the shadows. "I'm sorry I didn't get here in time," he said as he moved closer to Rikki. "I didn't know the General's plans until it was too late." Glancing around, he said, "We need to get out of here before someone sees us."

Motioning for them to follow, Jinx moved swiftly to where they'd left the SUV. Slipping behind the wheel, he waited for the rest of them to get in. Angel slid in the passenger seat while Phoenix and Nico sat in the second row holding Rikki and Ryker climbed in back. "How did you know where our truck was?" Phoenix asked suspiciously.

Turning to him, eyebrows raised Jinx asked, "Seriously? You have a team member bleeding out and you want to know how I found your vehicle?" Shaking his head in disgust, Jinx turned around and stepped on the gas pedal. "How about we worry about Rikki now and your useless excuse for an interrogation later."

Angel glanced back at Rikki, "How's she holding up?"

"She's in bad shape, boss," Nico responded quietly. "She's lost a lot of blood." Angel swore softly, the idea of losing one of her own breaking her heart.

"Jeremiah," Rikki whispered weakly. Oh shit, Angel thought. Jeremiah. He was going to go ape shit crazy if they lost Rikki. "Jeremiah," Rikki whispered again, a tear slipping down her cheek.

Jinx turned the SUV down a long dirt road heading away from the highway. Within a mile, they reached an abandoned barn. "What are we doing here, Jinx?" Angel asked in confusion. "We need to get to the plane. We have to get Rikki to Doc Josie now."

"She isn't going to make it to your doctor," Jinx replied as he opened the door. "Bring her in here." Not waiting for a response, Jinx left them and went to the barn. A small light shone through a window a few moments later.

"Let's go," Angel said as she slipped out of the vehicle, Nico and Phoenix following with Rikki.

"I'm staying outside," Ryker said as he pulled out his Glock. "I'll patrol the grounds until we leave." He was gone without a backward glance.

"What the hell are we doing here, Angel?" Phoenix demanded. "Rikki is going to die if we don't get her home now!"

"She will be dead before your plane touches the ground," Jinx said from the doorway. "She isn't strong enough to fight this kind of injury. She doesn't have the healing capabilities as a human to fight the way she needs to fight if she wants to live."

"So why the hell did you bring us to a barn?" Phoenix growled.

Jinx took a long, thin box from his coat pocket. When he opened it, Angel got a quick glance of what looked like a small surgery kit containing clamps, a scalpel, and a needle, among other things. "I'm going to do some minor surgery and then we're going to change her," was Jinx's calm reply. "We are going to give her that edge she needs to fight and win."

"We can't change her, Jinx," Angel cut in quietly. "Only mates can change humans, and her mate isn't here."

"Not true," Jinx responded as he led them to a place in the back of the barn. Motioning for them to place Rikki on the hay piled in a corner, he lowered himself beside her. Glancing back at them, he said, "Mates can change humans, but so can Alphas if they are strong enough."

"Her mate will fucking gut you if you have sex with her," Nico snarled from where he crouched in front of Rikki, still holding the bandage to her neck.

Shaking his head in exasperation, Jinx leaned back on his heels and looked at them. "First of all, Alphas do not have to have sex with someone to change them. Second of all, what makes you think

I'm changing her? Angel is her Alpha, she will do it."

Angel froze. She'd never changed anyone in her life. Hell, she hadn't even known she could. And there was no way she was going to kill Rikki trying. Locking eyes with her, Jinx said, "She's dead if you don't try, Angel. I can do the surgery, but she won't make it if she isn't turned. I can't do it. If I did, she would always be connected to me in some way, and her mate could reject her. I'm not saying he would, but there is always that possibility. It has to be you."

Falling to her knees on the other side of Rikki, Angel clasped Rikki's hand with her own. Staring into her terrified gaze, Angel asked, "Is this what you want, Rikki? Do you want me to try and change you? It may not work. It may end up killing you instead."

"Already dying," Rikki gasped. "Can feel it. Trust you, Angel. Want to live. Want Jeremiah."

"You know Jeremiah's your mate?" Angel asked in surprise.

Closing her eyes weakly, Rikki rasped, "Yes." As she slowly slid into unconsciousness, Angel made the only decision she could. "Do it," she said.

After injecting Rikki with something to help with the pain, Jinx slowly removed the gauze on her neck. Angel watched in awe as her son painstakingly performed surgery in the back of an old abandoned barn.

Close to an hour later, Jinx leaned back wiping beads of sweat from his brow. "Ok," he said softly, "it's your turn now, Angel."

"I don't know what to do," Angel admitted as she reached out and softly stroked a hand down Rikki's pale cheek. Glancing at Jinx, she said, "I've never done anything like this before. How do you know this is even possible? Have you done it?

"No," Jinx said shaking his head. "But I know someone who has."

"And it worked?" Phoenix questioned from his seat on a hay bale near them. "The person that was changed lived and didn't go mad?"

"Yes, it worked," Jinx said as he checked Rikki's pulse. "You need to do this now, Angel," he told her. "I will guide you, but if you want to save your friend, you can't wait any longer."

Taking a deep breath, Angel leaned closer to Rikki. "Just tell me what to do."

"I will show you," Jinx said. As Angel was bombarded by images in her head, she unconsciously reached out to Chase needing his courage and support. She sighed when she felt it given freely, no questions asked. Surrounded by her mate's strength, Angel opened her mouth, letting her fangs drop. Hovering over Rikki's bare shoulder, she tightened her hold on the hand she still held, and bit down.

~

"I have to go," Jinx said over three hours later after checking Rikki one more time. "Get her home and watch her closely. She will be out for a few days. Don't be alarmed. That's what happened to the other person, too." Standing, Jinx slipped into his coat. "She's going to make it."

"Thank you," Angel said as she gazed down at Rikki. She would have lost her tonight if it hadn't been for Jinx. Hating to ask more of him, she said, "I need your help with something else, Jinx." At his questioning look, she went on, "One of my team was stolen tonight by the General. Her name's Storm. Can you let Jade know if you hear anything at all about where that bastard might be keeping her? I want her back."

Nodding, he said, "Yeah, I'll see what I can find out and get in touch with Jade."

"Jinx," Angel called as he went to leave. Stopping, he waited. "Who taught you that?" she asked. "I had no idea it was even possible."

Looking back, Jinx seemed to be debating something before he finally said, "The same person who has taught me almost everything I know. My father." Then he vanished before Angel could respond.

"Angel," Nico said as he walked up beside her. "Angel, we need to go." Angel couldn't move, couldn't respond. Jinx said his father taught him everything he knew. No, that couldn't be right. His father was dead. The General had killed him years ago. Hadn't he?

Chapter 18

Jade sat in a seat in the back of the plane waiting for Angel to arrive. She'd tried several times to connect with Rikki, but was unable to, and it scared the hell out of her. "We need to call Jeremiah," she said as Trace sat down next to her. "He needs to know what's going on."

"Shit," Trace swore as he ran a hand tiredly over his head. "That's not a phone call I want to make."

"She cares for him," Jade whispered. "She will want him there when we get home."

Covering her hand with his, Trace promised, "We'll call him as soon as we know how she is, baby." Bringing her hand up and kissing her knuckles, he asked, "You ready to meet my family yet?"

Shaking her head, Jade leaned her head back and turned to gaze out the window. "Not right now, Trace."

As they sat there in silence, Jade thought about Rikki and everything she'd been through lately. From what Jade knew, Rikki had a rough life growing up. She'd never asked for specifics, but sometimes when she was near Rikki, she projected her thoughts loudly and it was hard to block them out. But over the past year, Jade had gotten to know Rikki better than anyone else on the team. She loved her snarky, sarcastic attitude. She admired her courage and fortitude. And Jade considered Rikki a friend. She was really the first and only friend Jade had ever had, unless you considered Flame. But Flame was too dead set on revenge to really become a good friend to anyone.

Hearing the sound of a vehicle, Jade jumped to her feet and stumbled over Trace. Running down the aisle on the plane, she raced out the door and down the stairs, stopping at the bottom to wait for the SUV to get there. When they pulled up, Nico slid out of the passenger seat, opening the door behind him. Reaching in, he guided a stunned looking Angel to the plane, shaking his head when anyone would have asked questions.

Pain squeezing her heart, Jade swung her gaze to where Phoenix opened the driver's side door and stepped out. Opening the door behind the driver's seat, he gathered Rikki in his arms and carried her to the plane. Quickly following them up the stairs, Jade paused in confusion. "You were with Jinx?" she asked, catching her brother's scent on Rikki.

"Your brother saved Rikki's life," Angel said from her seat at the front of the plane. "If it wasn't for him, she wouldn't be here now."

"She's different," Jade whispered. "You changed her."

"I had to. It was the only way to save her." Angel responded. "Although, I didn't even know that was possible. I thought only mates could change humans."

Shaking her head, Jade said, "Alphas can, too. Strong Alphas."

'So I learned," Angel muttered. Jade stiffened when Angel's angry eyes met hers. "So, tell me Jade. Did you learn that from Jinx or from your father?"

When Jade didn't respond, Angel continued, "Because from what Jinx told me, he learned it from your father. A father that I presumed was not only dead, but had been dead for the past 24 years."

Jade's breath caught in her throat. Seeing the anguish on Angel's face, Jade was unsure how to respond. Shaking her head, Angel turned away. "You know what? Keep your damn secrets. I don't fucking care anymore."

"Angel," Jade said hesitantly. When she refused to respond, Jade slowly walked over to her.

Reaching out, Jade rested a hand on her mother's shoulder. Pulling away from her, Angel told her coldly, "Go find a seat, Jade. We need to get Rikki home."

Fighting tears at the sting of her mother's rejection, Jade whispered, "I'm sorry. I wanted to tell you, but I couldn't. I've never met my father. All I know is the General didn't kill him. He keeps him locked up somewhere like he did me, except the General does experiments on him. Jinx won't tell me anymore than that."

Ignoring everyone else on the plane, Jade slowly made her way back to Rikki. She'd just lost her mother, which meant she'd probably lost the support of the whole team. What did that mean with Trace? Did she lose her mate too? Huddling up on the floor next to Rikki, Jade pulled her knees up and wrapped her arms tightly around them. Resting her head on her knees, she let her tears flow freely.

Hearing a growl, Jade looked up to see a very pissed off Trace. He'd shifted to his panther form, and letting out a huge roar, he let everyone know how angry he was. Baring his teeth in Angels direction, he roared again. Starr stood up and went to his side, standing in front of Angel.

"You told me earlier that I should stop and think before I opened my mouth when I was upset with Trace. Maybe you should do the same thing," Starr told Angel. "Just hours before you were prepared to defend your daughter, now you are mean and cruel to her? Why don't you ask her why she didn't tell you about her father instead of pushing her away?" Shaking her head, Starr turned from Angel and went to sit back down.

Letting out another threatening growl, Trace made his way back to Jade, curling up next to her. Sliding down, Jade rested her head on Trace's side and slowly fell asleep, letting go of the emotional misery for now.

Chapter 19

As soon as the plane touched down in Denver, Nico came to the back and squatted down next to Jade. Keeping an eye on Trace, he said quietly, "Give her time, Jade. She just found you not too long ago, then she finds out that the son she thought died at birth is really alive. And now she finds out a man she used to care deeply for, the father of her children, is being held by the General and being experimented on. She just needs time. She'll come around." Lifting Rikki into his arms, Nico stood up and walked down the aisle and out the door.

Jade waited until everyone was off the plane before standing up. Running a hand through her hair, she tiredly looked down at Trace. "I suppose you are upset with me, too?" she asked softly.

In moments, Trace was shifted and tugging her into his arms. "No, sweetheart, I'm not upset with you." Slipping a finger under her chin, he tilted her head back so he could look in her eyes. "Jade, I have spent my entire life holding secrets inside to protect others. Believe me when I say, I will never be upset with your for withholding information that could get someone else killed."

Smiling at Trace, Jade let her love for him shine through for him to see. She couldn't believe she'd found a mate as kind and understanding as he was fiercely protective. Slipping her arms around his neck she touched her lips softly to his. Pulling back at his low groan, she whispered, "We need to go with Rikki to the hospital, Trace. And we need to see how Gypsy and Sari are."

"Yeah," Trace grunted as he tugged on her hair with a grimace. "We also need to figure out if I still have an apartment. And what we are going to do with my mother and sister." Reaching up, he opened the compartment above the seat and pulled out some clothes. "Good thing we keep this plane well stocked," he chuckled. "I seem to be going through a lot of clothes lately."

"You're moving around easier," Jade observed as she followed him down the aisle after he dressed.

"The shifting helps," he said, "but it tires me out. And my legs are killing me."

"The doctor said they would for a while, but eventually you will be fine," Jade commented as her eyes strayed to his ass. Damn, it was a nice ass. Her hands itched to touch it, to caress it. Feeling a blush steal over her face as he stopped and looked at her, she shrugged. "What?"

"I don't know, you tell me," he growled. "I can smell your lust and it's driving me crazy. I don't know if we're going to make it off this plane without me taking you."

"We have to," Jade squeaked, taking a small step back. "They're waiting for us."

"Let them wait," Trace spit out right before he grabbed her and yanked her up against him. Jade gasped as she felt his hard length push against her thigh. Moaning, she pulled his lips down to hers, quickly opening her mouth to allow him access.

"Can you at least wait until we get to the White River Wolves' compound?" Jaxson asked dryly from the doorway. When Trace turned a dangerous look his way letting a low rumble work its way up his chest, Jaxson held up his hands with a smirk and backed slowly away. "We'll wait in the SUV for you," he said on a laugh.

Letting a small smile escape, Jade said, "Maybe we should get going." Reluctantly, she pulled back from Trace and gently pushed him toward the door, giggling at the pained expression he threw her way.

Leaving the plane and making her way down the steps outside, Jade glanced up and froze when she caught Angel's gaze. Making herself continue, she hesitated when she reached the pavement below, glancing in Angel's direction again. Forcing herself to hold back her tears as her mother turned away and got in the first waiting SUV, Jade followed Jaxson to the second one. Ryker sat in the passenger seat with Sophia and Starr in the very back, so she slid in the middle row with Trace. The ride to the compound was a quiet one, everyone preoccupied with their own thoughts.

When they reached the hospital, Chase was waiting for them on the front steps. As they exited the vehicle, Jade was once again engulfed in fear. Would her Alpha make her leave since she had managed to piss off his mate? God, she growled to herself, when did she become such a pansy? She'd lived her whole life without an Alpha. If Chase sent her away now, it would be no different. However, the ache in her chest said it would be.

Stopping in front of them, Chase glanced over to the other SUV where Doc Josie insisted on looking Rikki over before moving her into the hospital. Angel looked over, her eyes landing on Jade, before coldly looking away. The tension between the two women was obvious.

Looking back at Jade, Chase lifted an eyebrow inquiringly. Stiffening her shoulders she told him, "Angel just found out my father is still alive. I kept it from her because I was trying to protect him, and because Jinx told me to. The General has him." Her voice catching she finished softly, "She doesn't want to be around me because I have too many secrets." Holding her head high, her bottom lip quivering, she waited for Chase to tell her to leave. Instead, he stepped forward and gently touched her shoulder. Jade sighed, her whole body trembling when she felt his power seeping into her. "I'm sure she just needs time to digest it, Jade. Until then, you are more than welcome to stay here. Both of you," he said, including Trace. "Your family is welcome, too, Trace. I have two open apartments. When everyone is ready, I will have one of my enforcers take you to them."

"Thank you," Trace said gratefully, shaking Chase's hand. "Thank you for making my family and mate feel welcome." Jade didn't miss the glare he sent in Angel's direction.

"Jade's pack," Chase responded. "She will always be welcome on my lands." With one last gentle squeeze of Jade's shoulder, he was gone. Jade watched him head back to his office. He looked so alone. Sighing deeply, she laced her fingers with Trace's and they followed Sophia and Starr up the stairs and into the hospital.

Starr refused to be separated from her mother, so the nurses took them to the same room to wait for the doctor. After being held by Perez for the past couple of days while waiting for Trace to show, Trace insisted they be seen by Doc Josie. He knew his father hadn't been easy on them. The dark bruise on Starr's face was proof of that.

While Sophia and Starr were waiting to be seen, Jade and Trace went to Gypsy's room. She was sound asleep. "The poor woman hasn't woken up yet," a nurse said from the doorway. "It's almost as if she doesn't want to."

"Thank you," Jade said to the nurse. As soon as the nurse left, Jade turned to Trace. "Let me see what I can find out," Moving to the foot of the bed, Jade gently placed a hand on Gypsy's ankle. Closing her eyes, she slowly dropped her shields partway and let herself feel the emotions that were pouring out of Gypsy. Fear, pain, and confusion were at the forefront of her thoughts. *Come back, Gypsy,* Jade whispered into her mind. *Come back to us.*

I don't want to, Gypsy said. *Please don't make me. It hurts too much.*

Sending waves of peace and calm into the frightened woman, Jade responded, *You need to come back, Gypsy. Sari needs you.*

Sari? Gypsy asked in confusion. *Who's Sari?*

Sari, your sister. You do remember your sister, don't you? Jade questioned gently.

I don't have a sister, Gypsy said. *At least, I don't think I have a sister. I...I don't know. I can't remember. I don't remember anything.*

Breathing deeply, Jade slowly connected with Gypsy, but all she saw was a lost, scared woman. Gypsy wasn't lying. She had no idea who Sari was. She had no idea who she was. Slowly easing back out of Gypsy's mind, Jade whispered, *Come back to us. There's no reason to be afraid. I will give you all the answers you are seeking.*

Opening her eyes, Jade looked at Trace. "She has no idea who she is, who Sari is. She's so scared." Moving to the head of the bed, she placed a hand gently on Gypsy's swollen face. "Come back to us, Gypsy," she ordered softly. "It's time for you to come back."

As she watched, Gypsy's eyelids began to flutter. After a few moments, Jade was looking into her dark, pain filled gaze as tears streamed down her cheeks. "She needs more pain medicine," Jade told Trace, not taking her gaze from Gypsy's. Trace went to the door and hollered for a nurse.

"Can I help you?" the nurse asked as she entered the room.

"She needs more pain medicine," Jade told her. When the nurse didn't move right away, Jade growled, "Now!" Jumping, the nurse ran from the room.

Trace moved forward to stand by Jade's side, slipping an arm around her waist.

"Do you remember me, Gypsy?" Trace asked quietly. Gypsy shook her head no, grimacing slightly at the pain the movement caused. Trace's hand tightened on Jade's hip. "What's the last thing you remember?" he asked.

Jade watched in sympathetic silence as Gypsy fought to remember. After several moments she whispered, "Nothing. I don't remember anything." Looking up at them, she whispered, "Why can't I remember anything? Why do I hurt so much? God, everything hurts."

Jade pushed more calming vibes Gypsy's way to try and keep her calm. "It's okay, Gypsy," she said with a small smile, "your memory will come back. You've been through a lot and you just need some rest."

Nodding weakly, the frightened woman lay back against her pillow, gazing around the room uncertainly. "Where am I?"

"You're at the hospital and you are safe," Doc Josie said as she made her way into the room. "I'm Doc Josie and I'm going to take care of you."

Glancing at Trace and Jade, the doctor gestured towards the door, "Why don't you go and get some rest. Sari's asleep right now and will be for some time. I'm going to talk to Gypsy for a few minutes and then she's going to get some rest, also. You can come back tomorrow if you would like."

"Are they going to be alright, Doc," Trace asked as he let go of Jade's hip and took her hand in his.

"They will both be fine after some time," Josie responded. "We can discuss it at more length tomorrow. Don't think I have overlooked the fact that you have pushed yourself to the limit, Trace. You are obviously in pain and exhausted. Now go get some rest before I admit you back into the hospital."

"I'm going, Doc," Trace agreed tiredly, "but we have to wait for my mom and Starr." When they reached the doorway, Jade turned back. "What about Rikki?" she asked. "Is she going to be okay?"

"She's alive," the doctor said, "but I've never heard of anyone doing what your mother did. We will have to wait to see how it turns out."

Nodding, Jade slipped her hand in Trace's and they went to the waiting room to rest while they waited for Sophia and Starr. Jade sat in a chair by Trace, leaning her head against the wall. She was so exhausted. Letting her eyes drift shut, she slipped into a light sleep feeling overwhelmed by everything that had happened in the past few days.

Chapter 20

Glaring at the paperwork on his desk, Chase tried to get control of his anger. It was hard to do when right now all he wanted to do was to pick up his huge desk and heave it through the window.

Clenching his hands into tight fists, he fought to control his breathing and calm himself. Hearing a noise at the door, he glanced up and bared his fangs at the intrusion. Slade, Chase's head enforcer, held his hands up and slowly backed away. "You called me, Chase," he reminded his Alpha. "You want me to come back later?"

Shaking his head, Chase tried again to control his ragged breathing. "I need you to go over to the hospital and show Trace and his family to their new apartments. I'm giving them the ones on the south end right across from each other."

"Shit, you keep bringing in strays and we are going to run out of room," Slade joked lightly.

Lifting his head, Chase snarled, "Then we will build another damn building. Now get out!"

Eyes widening, Slade quickly turned and left, shutting the door behind him.

Chase pushed his chair back and stood. He fought, unsuccessfully, to push down the darkness that threatened to consume him. The father of Angel's children was alive. The man that his mate had once loved, possibly still loved.

Chase had waited months for Angel to realize they would be better together. That he would love and support her the way every mate deserved. But she'd refused him, again and again. Now he wondered if it was because of this other man. He wondered if she would ever truly be his.

Not able to control himself any longer, Chase knew he had to get out of the building now before he endangered one of his pack members. Quickly stripping off his clothes, he shifted into his huge black wolf. Letting out a howl of pure rage and pain, he flew through the large window in his office, breaking the glass and landing on the ground outside. After shaking the glass out of his fur, he howled again as he he took off across the land and into the woods at a run. Reaching the outside borders of his land, he kept going, deeper into the woods and up the mountain side on the back of his property, running until he could run no more. Stopping finally, he lay on the ground, his head on his paws. He couldn't go back to the compound yet. Soon, but not yet.

~

Hearing the sound of her mate in pain, Angel stopped the SUV on the way through the gates of the compound. Jumping out of the vehicle, she ran quickly toward the office building. The sound of glass breaking had several people following her. She ran faster when she heard Chase howl again. Clearing the corner of the building, she stopped as she watched him tearing off across the terrain. He was gorgeous and majestic and full of so much anguish that it brought her to her knees. Letting out a soft cry, she wrapped her arms tightly around herself and let his agony wash over her.

She was causing him this pain. She could feel it. When she tried to connect with him, he blocked her. Shocked, she slowly staggered to her feet. Ignoring the concerned gazes of the people around her, she stumbled back to the SUV, crawling in and slamming the door shut. Leaving the compound, Angel went straight home. Pulling out a bottle of wine, she went straight to the bathroom. After filling her large tub with water, she tossed in some bath salts. Turning her radio on high, she climbed in the scalding hot water. As George Straight crooned in the background, Angel screamed loudly at the injustice that life was throwing her way lately.

Yanking the cork out of the bottle of wine, she took a large drink, not bothering with a glass. Taking another drink she thought about how screwed up her life was. She'd met her mate, but refused to claim him. She'd finally gotten her daughter back, only to push her out of her life today. She'd found out the son she'd been told had died 24 years ago, was really alive. Now she was being told, the man she'd trusted so many years ago, one she thought had betrayed her, was also still alive. Not only was he alive, but he was being tortured and experimented on by a sadistic son of a bitch that had orchestrated all of the hell in her life. And to top it off, Chase was gone. Her mate was gone, and she was alone, once again.

Resting her head back against the top of the bathtub, Angel let the tears flow. After taking another drink of her wine, she threw the bottle across the bathroom, smashing it against the far wall. Shattered, she thought as she stared at it. Just like her life.

Chapter 21

Jade's heart was breaking for her Alpha. She'd not only heard his gut wrenching pain, but she'd also felt it bone deep. And now she understood what it was about. She wanted to kick herself for telling Chase about her father the way she had. She hadn't been thinking about how he would feel when he found out Angel's old flame was still alive. She'd only been thinking about herself and what would happen if she was removed from the White River Compound.

Jade wanted to follow Chase. She needed to explain to him that what happened between her father and Angel years ago, the love they may have felt for each other, was nothing compared to what Chase and Angel could have now. They were mates, and the bond between mates was never broken. When she tried to go to him, though, Trace stopped her. "You need to let him be for a while," he said. "Chase left on purpose. He could hurt someone in his condition."

"He's right," a voice interrupted when she would have protested. "I don't know what happened, but Chase isn't thinking clearly right now. He's letting his emotions get the best of him and he could easily hurt someone. The best thing he could have done is leave. He will be back when he's ready."

Looking over, Jade took in the tall, dark haired, muscular man standing in the doorway of the waiting room where she and Trace were still sitting. They'd been there for a full hour, but she knew Doc Josie was trying to take care of several patients at once. Sophia and Starr were the less injured of them all, so they would be seen last.

"Hey Slade," Trace said as he got up and bumped fists with the man. "What's going on?"

"Chase sent me to show you and your mate your new digs," Slade said with a grin. "He said you have a mother and sister, too?" he questioned with a glance around the room.

"They're in with Doc Josie," Trace responded, gesturing towards the first room. "I thought they would be done by now."

Suddenly, the door opened and Sophia and Starr emerged with Doc Josie. Smiling, Josie told them goodbye and went into the room next to theirs. Smiling, his mother came over and gently hugged Trace. "She said we are fine," Sophia told them.

"Just like we tried to tell you," Starr grumbled.

Trace grinned and introduced them to Slade. "Slade is going to show us to our new homes for the time being," he said.

"New homes?" Sophia asked hopefully. "We are going to live by you?"

"Right across from him, actually," Slade laughed. "You can drive each other crazy like family is supposed to."

Happiness filling Sophia's eyes, she turned to Jade. "This means so much to me." Gently taking hold of Jade's hand, Sophia said, "Welcome to my family, Jade. I am so happy to meet you."

"Thank you," Jade said, lightly squeezing Sophia's fingers.

"I will never forget what you did for me, Jade," Sophia told her, tears shining in her eyes. "Thank you for protecting me from Philip."

"I will always protect you," Jade vowed. "Both of you," she said including Starr.

Smiling, Trace pulled Jade close, kissing her softly. "We better find our new homes so we can get some rest. I think we all need it." Jade shivered at the heat in his gaze, blushing when Slade laughed.

Motioning for them to follow him, Slade left the waiting area. As he stepped toward the doors, Slade stopped suddenly. Cocking his head to the side, he breathed in deeply, his eyes widening in surprise.

"What is it?" Trace asked, stepping in front of Jade to protect her. Not answering, Slade moved quickly past him and down the hall before stopping in front of Gypsy's door. Resting a hand lightly on the doorjamb, he watched her sleep.

"Stay here with your family, Trace," Jade said as she stepped around him. When he would have protested, Jade shook her head. "I will be fine, but you need to stay here for now. Please." Reluctantly, Trace let her go, but continued to stand in the doorway of the waiting room watching.

Jade quietly approached Slade, stopping just behind him. "What happened to her," he growled, taking in Gypsy's broken arm and bruised features.

"She was held by Trace's father, a Colombian drug lord, in horrible conditions for months," Jade told Slade softly as she moved to stand next to him. "She and Trace were both starved and beaten repeatedly. She's been through a lot and has lost her memory. Personally, I think she is suppressing it so she doesn't have to remember everything she has endured." As Slade's hand tightened on the jamb, she went on, "If she is who I think she is to you, Slade, please, give her time. She will remember. Gypsy is a fighter. She fought for my mate. If it wasn't for her courage, he might not be here today."

Slowly Slade entered the room and made his way to Gypsy's bedside. Reaching out, he rested a gentle hand on her head, before slowly sliding it down her long dark hair. Gypsy's eyes fluttered open and came to rest on Slade's face. At first fear filled her gaze, but then her eyes widened and she asked quietly, "Do I know you?"

"No," Slade told her, shaking his head. "Not yet." Softly tracing a finger down her cheek he whispered, "Get some rest, Gypsy."

As Gypsy drifted back to sleep, a soft smile on her lips, Jade felt hope rise in her. Gypsy had a mate. A strong mate who would help her get through this dark part in her life. She was going to make it, Jade had no doubt.

Seeing Doc Josie coming their way, Jade raised a finger to her lips. Nodding in Slade's direction, she said, "Looks like Gypsy won't have to go through this alone."

Eyeing them with concern, Josie motioned for Jade to follow her. Taking Jade to her office, Josie sat at her desk while Jade took a seat in one of the chairs in front of it. "Is Slade Gypsy's mate?" she asked.

Nodding, Jade smiled. "Yes, he is"

"From what I know, Slade was married once before over 100 years ago," Josie said frowning. "His wife wasn't his true mate, but he loved her and chose to marry for love instead of waiting for his fated mate. His wife died during child birth along with the baby. Slade was devastated. He hasn't shown interest in anyone since. Hopefully after all this time, he will be willing to open his heart to Gypsy."

"He will," Jade promised. "It might take a while, but it is starting to happen already. I can feel it."

"Jade," Doc Josie said hesitantly as she eyed her curiously. "Why do you insist on being a part of RARE? It seems to me like you would be happier doing something else."

"Like what?" Jade questioned. "I don't really know anything else. Although, I used to spend some time in the labs at the facility where I was held in Arizona. A couple of the scientists let me help with their experiments. I don't really feel like that's something I would enjoy either, though."

"Actually," Doc Josie began tentatively, "I have something else in mind."

"You do?" Josie asked hopefully.

"I would like you to consider working here at the hospital. "You are a very kind and caring person, and that's what we need here. Also, your ability to help calm others would be a big asset." At Jade's surprised gasp, the doctor laughed. "Did you think I didn't notice what you have done for so many people in this hospital already? I won't pretend to fully understand how your ability works, but I would love to have you as a part of my staff."

"I'm not an Omega wolf," Jade said, looking Doc Josie in the eyes. It was important that the doctor realize this, because Jade refused to pretend anymore.

"No, Jade, you aren't," Josie agreed. "Omegas are submissive. Their mere presence alone can calm an entire pack. You simply choose the people that need you the most and help them. And I would never call you submissive. You have too much of your mother's personality. The difference is that you don't want to be an Alpha. Your great passion is helping others. Not asserting your authority."

Nodding, Jade responded, "I love to help others. I hate to see anyone in pain." Crossing her arms over her chest she whispered, "I hate killing. It hurts."

"That's because you are a healer, Jade, not a fighter." Standing, Doc Josie smiled down at her. "You think about it and let me know. If you are agreeable, I would like to get you enrolled in some online college classes. It's wonderful that you are able to help people with your gift, but I want you to better understand exactly why they feel the way they do and other methods of helping them as well. I would like your role here to be similar to that of a counselor."

"When would I start," Jade asked, still in shock that the doctor wanted her to work at the hospital. Jinx told her it was time to be the person she wanted to be. This was what she wanted. To be able to help others in a healing capacity was the perfect thing for her.

"As soon as possible," Doc Josie said. "Gypsy and Sari will both need someone to help them, as well as Rikki. I'm not sure what is going to happen when she wakes."

Looking down at her tightly clasped hands, Jade said, "Thank you, Doc. Thank you so much for giving me this opportunity." Glancing up, Jade smiled. "I need some rest and time with my mate. I can start the day after tomorrow."

"Perfect," Josie said. "Meet with me first thing so we can go over the patients' charts. I will let you know about the classes."

As she started to leave, Jade called out, "Wait. How will I be able to take classes?" Tears welling up in her eyes, she whispered, "I don't have any paperwork…"

"You leave all of that to me," Josie assured her. "I will make it happen. Now, we better get back before Trace starts getting antsy."

Leaving Josie's office, they walked back to Gypsy's room, but Slade was gone. In the waiting room they found Trace talking with his mother and Starr. Spotting them, he asked. "You ready? Slade said he would meet us outside."

"Yes," Jade said, unable to contain the grin of delight on her face. "Let's go. I have something to talk to you about."

Walking over, Trace slipped an arm around her waist and kissed her softly on the lips. "You ready?" he asked Sophia and Starr. They stood by the window, arms wrapped around each other.

Taking a deep breath, Sophia nodded. "Let's go see our new home."

Together, they left and met Slade in front of the hospital. Following him to the apartments, Jade could tell he was lost in thought and not ready for any kind of interaction with others. When Trace would have tried to pull Slade into a conversation, Jade grabbed his arm and shook her head.

After Slade showed Sophia and Starr to their two bedroom apartment, he took Trace and Jade through their one bedroom. Taking pity on him, Jade said, "Thank you, Slade. We really appreciate everything." Opening the door, she smiled, "I will be by to see Gypsy in a couple of days. Maybe I will see you there?"

Meeting her gaze for the first time since they left the hospital, Slade nodded, "Yeah…yeah, I might be there." With a goodbye to Trace, Slade left in a daze. Jade sighed as she shut the door behind him.

"What's wrong with him?" Trace asked as he walked up behind Jade, sliding his arms around her waist and resting his chin on her shoulder. Leaning her head back, Jade locked her arm around the back of his head, pulling it into her neck, moaning softly as he licked at her mate bite. "He found his mate," she responded, tightening her fingers in his head and holding him to her. "He will need to have patience with her."

Lifting his head, Trace's eyes narrowed, "Gypsy?"

"Yes," Jade growled, pulling his head back down to her shoulder. "He is going through some issues and needs some time to think. Your mom and sister need time to rest. I need to feel my mate deep inside me. How about we give everyone what they need?"

Groaning, Trace grabbed her hips, pulling her back against him, before gently nipping around her mate bite. Her breath quickened as she felt him lick up her neck and gently bite down on her ear. He was driving her insane. "Please," she moaned, pushing back against his hard length. "Please."

Picking her up, Trace made his way quickly to the bedroom. After laying her gently on the bed, he stepped back and slowly started to remove his clothing. Jade gulped as he slid his shirt up and off, exposing his gorgeous body to her greedy gaze. She wanted to trail her fingers down his chest and over his muscular abs. She was going to lick every inch of him. Dropping his shirt to the floor, Trace slid his hands to his jeans. Jade panted softly as he slowly unbuttoned them. *Mine,* she thought, *Mine.*

Laughing quietly, Trace pushed them down, his cock springing free. Jade growled, she wanted a taste now. "Not yet," Trace said as he removed his jeans and then his socks. "Lay back," he ordered roughly.

When she would have removed her clothes quickly, he shook his head. "No, that's for me to do." Her eyes widening, Jade lay back against the pillows and waited. She didn't have long to wait. Trace lowered himself to the bed beside her, and reached out to softly rub a finger over her lips. Leaning forward, he captured them with his mouth, tracing them with his tongue. She felt his hand move under the front of her shirt, sliding up to cup her breast through her bra. Tweaking the nipple, he laughed when she squeaked. "Oh God," she moaned when he slipped his tongue inside her mouth, tangling it with hers.

Jade gasped as she felt his hand move from her breast down her stomach. She waited impatiently as Trace undid the button of her jeans and would have pushed them off, but he grabbed her hands. Holding them above her head, he growled, "Don't move."

Jade watched through hooded eyes as Trace slid down her body. After removing her jeans, he kissed his way back up to the top of her panties. Slowly pulling them down, he leaned forward and licked her clit. Jade jumped and a small cry escaped. "Trace," she begged. "Please, Trace, I need you. I can't wait any longer." Licking again, he ignored her. Moaning, Jade reached down and grabbed his head, moving her hips and rubbing against his mouth. As Trace played her with his tongue, Jade panted loudly. Feeling her orgasm building, Jade pressed him tighter against her and cried out as she came.

Moving quickly, Trace prowled back up her body. Slipping her shirt over her head and removing her bra, he leaned back, his whole body shaking. "I need you, Jade. I don't know if I can be gentle."

"Do it," Jade growled. Digging her nails into his shoulder, she reared up and slammed her mouth to his. He groaned and took over the kiss, rough and demanding. Suddenly, Trace pulled back and flipped Jade onto her stomach. Pulling her hips up, he pushed her shoulders down into the bed before slowly burying himself deeply inside her. "Oh God," she cried as she felt him stretching her. He tried to stop when he was all of the way in, but Jade didn't want him to. Pushing back against him, she demanded, "Move, dammit!"

Still holding her shoulders down with one hand, Trace grabbed her hip with his other one and held her still while he pulled out and slammed back into her. "Yes," she moaned. "More, Trace, more!" She needed to feel him moving inside of her. Needed to bond with him again.

Reaching down between them, Jade cupped his balls and gently tugged on them. "Fuck," he groaned as he moved faster. Trace moved the hand from her back and slipped it around to her mound. The feel of his fingers on her clit was too much and Jade screamed as she came again. Snarling, Trace leaned forward and bit her shoulder, claiming her again as he came.

Licking the bite, Trace slowly pulled back and lay down on his side, tugging Jade up against him. Kissing her softly on the neck he said, "I love you, Jade."

Closing her eyes tiredly, Jade whispered, "I love you too.

Chapter 22

Feeling the warm male body wrapped around hers, Jade smiled as she opened her eyes. She wasn't sure what time it was, but by the sunlight filtering through the room, she figured it was close to noon the following day. Turning around in Trace's arms, Jade slowly traced his features with her fingers. He was so sexy. She loved how caring and protective he was. Kissing him tenderly, she grinned as he growled, "There better be more than that coming, woman."

Opening his eyes, he laughed. "What has you in such a good mood today?" he asked as he rubbed a hand up and down her back nudging her closer.

Feeling his erection pressed hard against her stomach, Jade moaned softly. "I'm happy, Trace. I'm so damn happy. I have you, I'm free and I have a job!"

"A job," he asked in bewilderment. "You mean with RARE?"

"No," Jade said excitedly. Cupping his cheek in her palm she said, "Jinx told me I am free to be who I want to be, Trace. I don't have to pretend to be anyone I'm not. I don't have to be who Jinx made me, I don't have to be the person I have been pretending to be for as long as I can remember. I can be me! And I finally figured out who that is."

"I know exactly who you are," Trace said as he dropped a soft kiss on her forehead. "You are one of the sweetest, gentlest, kindest females I know. Yes, you can kick ass if and when you need to, but that's not you, love."

"No," Jade agreed, "it's not." Sitting up, she looked down at Trace. Her eyes shining with happiness, she said, "I'm a healer, Trace. I want to help people. I want to be the one they talk to when they have problems. I want to be there to help them fight their pain, whether it is physical or emotional. Doc Josie offered me a job at the hospital, Trace. I will get to be who I really want to be and do something I love."

Jade giggled as Trace lifted her on top of him, sitting her over the top of his thick, hard cock. "That's wonderful, baby," he growled as he slid her down over him, pushing as far inside her as he could go. Taking over, Jade rose up and then slowly slid back down onto him. "Oh, yeah, baby," he rasped. "Just like that." Keeping a steady pace, Trace let her be in charge for just a short time. Suddenly losing control, he grabbed her hips tightly and took over. God she loved how good he felt inside her. In no time, she was screaming his name as she sank her fangs into his shoulder. Feeling him burst inside of her, she let herself go.

Snuggling into Trace afterwards, Jade said softly, "Everything would be perfect if Angel didn't hate me and Jinx was here."

Gently stroking a hand down her long hair, Trace kissed her softly. "Angel doesn't hate you, Jade. She's upset and hurt, but she doesn't hate you. She's your mother, she loves you. She just needs to wrap her mind around everything. I promise you, she will come around."

"I hope so," Jade said. "I wish I had done things differently, Trace. I really do. But I thought I was doing the right thing at the time. Jinx told me about my father in confidence. I never want to give my brother a reason not to trust me. Instead, I gave my mother one."

Nuzzling her cheek, Trace replied, "You did what you had to do. You protected your brother and your father. Angel will come to realize that. She just needs time. As for Jinx, something tells me he can take care of himself. We will be here to help if he needs us, though. He's family, Jade."

Holding him close, Jade whispered, "I love you so damn much, Trace."

"Me too, baby, me too," Trace murmured.

They lay like that for a few minutes before Jade reluctantly pulled back. "We need to get dressed and eat. We should go see your family today, Trace. They will want to spend some time with you."

Nodding, Trace groaned as he slid out of bed and stood. "Stay there," he ordered. Jade smiled to herself as he went and turned on the shower. She really enjoyed how much Trace wanted to take care of her. It made her feel loved. Finally, everything in her life seemed to be working out. Well, almost everything.

Jade squealed when Trace came back into the room and scooped her up off the bed. After depositing her into the shower, he climbed in after her and proceeded to clean her from head to toe.

Chapter 23

Over an hour later, finally showered, clothed and fed, Trace and Jade knocked on the door across the hall. A smiling Sophia greeted them both with a hug, and opening the door wide, she invited them in.

"I am so glad you came to see us today," Sophia said as she motioned them to take a seat on the couch. "Trace, there is something I wanted to give you. It is very special to me. I managed to keep it hidden from Philip for years. I've been saving it for you, but couldn't give it to you until I knew for sure we were free."

Rushing from the room, Sophia came back just a few minutes later and stood in front of Trace. "I managed to grab it as we left the last house before coming here. It was in the living room, in a drawer." Opening her hand, she showed Trace the dog tags. Rubbing her finger over the words engraved on them, she whispered, "These were your great grandfather's. His side of the family is where you get your ability to shift. For some reason, I have never been able to, but a handful of the people in our family always could." Placing the dog tags in his hand, she smiled tremulously. "All of our family is gone now, son, except you. You will carry on his legacy. You and Jade."

Trace lightly ran his fingers over the name, Anthony Cordell. His great grandfather. "How did you keep this from Perez?" he asked.

"I was wearing it when he captured me. Somehow he missed it. When he took me to his home, he left me alone in his room for hours before he came to me. I hid it, and I changed the hiding place daily. It was the only thing I had left of my family. I refused to let him take it from me too. When we escaped, I wore it once again." Tears filling Sophia's eyes she said, "I can't believe he is finally gone. I don't have to watch for him around every corner."

Clasping the dog tags tightly in his hand, Trace stood. Gathering his mother in his arms, he told her, "I will wear them proudly, Mother. And I will pass them on to my own son or daughter someday."

"Good," Sophia said happily, "that is very good." Taking the chain from him, Sophia slipped it up over his head. Patting his chest where the tags rested, she smiled. "This is where they belong." Backing up, she included Jade, "Now, come and have a snack. When Starr gets out of the shower, we will all go for a walk. We need to get to know our new home."

"We just ate," Trace laughed as his mother pulled him into the kitchen.

"You need to eat a lot more. You are too skinny," Sophia insisted. "You need to be strong so you can keep your pretty mate safe."

Shaking his head, Trace sat down at the table. Reaching over, he snagged Jade's wrist and pulled her to him, settling her onto his lap. Jade slipped an arm around his shoulders and laughed as his mother filled the table with food. Both of their apartments had come stocked. Most of his mother's supply looked like it was now in front of him.

For the rest of the day, Trace and Jade spent time with Trace's family, shopping for clothes they were all in desperate need of. They also stopped by the hospital to check on Gypsy, Sari and Rikki, but found they were all sleeping.

That night was filled with laughter and joy as Trace and Jade settled into their new place. After dinner and some television, they decided to call it a night, falling asleep in each other's arms.

Chapter 24

Trace woke to the insistent knock on his door. Glancing around the room, he groaned at the dark hour. Rising, he pulled the covers back around Jade, before grabbing some sweats and yanking them on. After a quick look through the peep hole, Trace growled as he opened the door to a smiling Phoenix. "Rise and shine, cupcake," Phoenix laughed. "Angel called a meeting. If you had a phone, you would know that. Don't worry, though, Angel has one for ya."

"What the fuck time is it?" Trace snarled. This was not how he planned on waking up today. He wanted to spend the morning buried in his beautiful mate, not with his team.

"It's 5 in the morning, the meeting is at 6. That gives us just enough time to run through the golden arches on our way to Angel's," Phoenix smirked. "Come on, get dressed. Let's do this."

Slamming the door in Phoenix's face, Trace turned and went back into the bedroom. Rummaging through the dresser, he pulled out a new pair of jeans and a long sleeved top. "What are you doing?" Jade asked drowsily from the bed.

"Angel called a meeting. Fucking Phoenix is outside waiting for me," Trace growled as he got dressed. "I'm sorry, Jade. This isn't how I wanted to wake you up this morning."

"It's ok," came Jade's sleepy response. "You need to go. It's probably about Storm. You need to find her. I'm going to get up soon and go to the hospital."

"It's only 5, baby," Trace said as he kissed her softly, "Get some more sleep."

Snuggling back under the covers with a soft sigh, Jade whispered, "Love you."

"Love you, too," Trace told her as he stood up and left the bedroom. Grabbing a coat from the closet, he once again opened the front door. Phoenix was leaning up against the wall next to the door waiting. "Let's go," Trace snarled, softly shutting the door behind him.

Nico and Ryker were waiting outside in the back of a black, four door, Dodge Charger. Trace grinned, "New car?"

"Hell yeah," Phoenix smirked. "I got this baby just a couple of months ago. Glad I went with the four door since Serenity's pregnant."

"Serenity's pregnant?" Trace's grin grew. "Congrats, man!" he said bumping fists with Phoenix. "Hope I get that soon."

"It's the best feeling ever, T," Phoenix said as he slid into the driver's seat. Trace opened the passenger door, running his hand over the top of the slick Charger. He had missed out on so much the past few months. Getting in, Trace shut the door behind him and leaned back against the leather seats. Stretching out his legs as much as possible, he groaned softly. There was still some pain, and his legs were slightly stiff, but they were so much better than just the day before. Concentrating, Trace did some exercises on the way to Denver, stretching the muscles.

After driving through to grab some breakfast, they headed to Angel's. Pulling down her long drive, they saw Angel coming from the barn. "Shit," Phoenix said as he stopped the car in front of her house. "This isn't going to be good."

Getting out of the car, Trace noticed the blood smeared on Angel's knuckles. Walking up to her, he handed her a bag of breakfast burritos as a peace offering. "Don't get your fucking blood on my breakfast," he growled as he continued up the steps and into the house.

When they were all in the conference room in the basement they dug into breakfast while waiting for Angel to take a quick shower. Jaxson was set up on one end of the long table and looked like he'd been there for a while. "Don't you ever sleep, Jax?" Nico asked as he tossed him a sausage biscuit.

"Not when one of ours is missing," Jaxson responded, tearing into the food. "I've been up all night trying to figure out where the General would take Storm, but I'm coming up empty for the most part."

Entering the room, Angel asked, "Where's Jade?"

"Jade isn't a part of RARE anymore," Trace responded shortly before taking another bite of his food.

Angel stiffened. "Why not?"

"She got a better offer. One that suits her more than hunting and killing," was Trace's response. Taking a drink of his coffee, he continued, "She did tell me to let you know that Jinx said to get rid of the bike in your barn. He didn't exactly obtain it legally."

"It's already been taken care of," Flame said from the doorway. Nodding at them, she walked in and sat down, grabbing one of the burritos Angel left on the table. "What's this about Jade not being a part of RARE anymore?"

"Is this because of me?" Angel asked quietly as she took a seat by Flame.

"Actually, it has nothing to do with you. Doc Josie offered her a job at the hospital. Said Jade's a natural healer and thinks she will be a big help to the patients with her gifts. She even wants to have Jade take some online courses." Trace responded, grabbing a burrito and devouring it. Damn, he was hungry.

Nodding, Angel agreed, "She is. And it will be nice not to have to worry about her while out on missions."

"True," Trace said as he reached for another burrito.

"Shit man, leave some for the rest of us," Phoenix groused. Flipping him off, Trace tore off the wrapper and inhaled the food.

"Okay," Angel interrupted, "let's get this meeting going. First thing we need to discuss is Storm. We haven't heard from Jinx yet, so all we have to go on is a couple of facilities Jaxson found that the General has hidden deep. We are going to leave tonight to check the first one out. It's highly unlikely that's where Storm is from what Jax can tell, but until we find our girl, we are gonna go in hot on any and all facilities we can find."

"Oorah," Phoenix muttered from where he sat in the corner.

"I need you all on this. I'm not asking." Shrugging Angel said, "You would be insulted if I asked anyway."

"Damn straight," Ryker hissed. "Storm's ours. We're all going." It got loud as everyone voiced their agreement, then Angel held up a hand.

"The other thing I wanted to talk to you about today is Rikki," Angel continued after it quieted down. "I've spoken with Doc Josie and Rikki's still sleeping. The Doc has no idea how long Rikki will be out, but we may have another problem." Running a hand through her hair, Angel sighed heavily. "I've been trying to get a hold of Jeremiah since we got back. His phone goes directly to voice mail. Yesterday I called his office and got his secretary. She refused to say anything except that Jeremiah wasn't there. She did consent to have the director call me back, which he finally did this morning. It seems Jeremiah has been on an undercover mission of his own since July infiltrating a human trafficking organization. The FBI lost contact with him last November."

"Shit," Nico cursed. "That explains why they have you dealing with a different agent recently."

"Yeah, I thought it was because Jeremiah needed time away from Rikki," Angel growled, slamming her fist onto the table. "If I had known he might be in trouble I would have done something about it. I haven't been able to reach him the few times I've tried to connect with him, but he could be unconscious."

"The director agreed to let us do our own reconnaissance on the side," Jaxson cut in, "as long as we don't screw up the FBI's mission. I haven't found anything yet, but it could be that Jeremiah is so deep undercover that he has managed to hide from everyone."

"We are going to be very busy the next few weeks, people," Angel said as she stood from her chair. "I want you back here in full gear by 7 p.m. tonight. We head out to the first facility we found of the General's. If we can't find Storm, hopefully we will get a hit on where Jeremiah might be."

Before leaving, Angel turned to Trace, "Come upstairs with me, please, Trace. I have something for Jade." Not waiting, she left the room leaving Trace to follow.

"Meet us outside," Phoenix said as he finished off his last burrito. "I need to get back home and spend some time with Serenity before we leave."

Trace found Angel in her office, removing something from the safe. Handing it to him, she said, "This is Jade's birth certificate. She will need it if she is going to take classes."

"Thanks," Trace told her as he accepted the certificate. "You know, you could give this to her yourself, Angel. It would mean a lot to her."

"I just can't right now, Trace." Angel moved to sit at her desk, leaning back in her chair. "I love my daughter. I will always love her no matter what. But I need some time."

"She didn't do anything you wouldn't have done, Angel," Trace insisted. "You know damn well you would do whatever it takes to protect your family. That's all Jade was doing."

"I know," Angel agreed, rubbing her eyes tiredly. "I know this in my head, Trace, but my heart is having a hard time catching up. I just need some time."

"Fine," Trace said as he turned to leave. "Just don't take too much time, Angel. You and Jade have been separated far too long already. She's hurting just as much as you."

Trace went outside where Phoenix, Nico and Ryker waited, and they all piled into the Charger to go home. They had a long haul ahead of them, but RARE never left a teammate behind. They would hunt to the ends of the earth for Storm and Jeremiah, taking out any obstacles in their path.

Author Bio

I have a wonderful, supportive husband and three beautiful children. I enjoy spending time with all of them which normally involves some baseball, shooting hoops, taking walks, watching movies, and of course reading.

My passion for reading began at a very young age and only grew over time. Whether I was bringing home a book from the library, or sneaking one of my mom's romance novels and reading by the light in the hallway when we were supposed to be sleeping, I always had a book.

I read several different genres and subgenres, but Paranormal Romance and Romantic Suspense have always been my favorites

I have always made up my own stories, and have just recently decided to start sharing them. I hope everyone enjoys reading them as much as I enjoy writing them.

~~ Dawn

CPSIA information can be obtained
at www.ICGtesting.com
Printed in the USA
LVHW012209090119
603394LV00017B/1019/P

9 781502 864437